327314

4A/gv

SAINTS AND STRANGERS

Angela Carter was born in 1940; she published her first
novel, *Shadow Dance*, in 1965 and was immediately rec-
ognized as one of Britain's most original and disturbing
writers. Since then, she has written seven other novels,
three collections of short stories, two books of nonfic-
tion, a translation of the fairy tales of Charles Perrault,
and numerous poems and pieces of journalism. She is the
author of the screenplay for *The Company of Wolves*, a
fantasy film; a collection of her radio scripts was published in England in 1985. Angela Carter lives in London
but frequently teaches in the United States, most recently
at the University of Texas and at the Iowa Writers'
Workshop.

Saints and Strangers

ANGELA CARTER

A KING PENGUIN PUBLISHED BY PENGUIN BOOKS

PENGUIN BOOKS
Viking Penguin Inc., 40 West 23rd Street,
New York, New York 10010, U.S.A.
Penguin Books Ltd, 27 Wrights Lane, London W8 5TZ
(Publishing & Editorial) and Harmondsworth, Middlesex,
England (Distribution & Warehouse)
Penguin Books Australia Ltd, Ringwood,
Victoria, Australia
Penguin Books Canada Limited, 2801 John Street,
Markham, Ontario, Canada L3R 1B4
Penguin Books (N.Z.) Ltd, 182–190 Wairau Road,
Auckland 10, New Zealand

First published in Great Britain under the title *Black Venus* by
Chatto & Windus, Ltd 1985
First published in the United States of America by
Viking Penguin Inc. 1986
Published in Penguin Books 1987

This American edition contains a different version of
the story "The Fall River Axe Murders."

Page vi constitutes an extension of this copyright page.

LIBRARY OF CONGRESS CATALOGING IN PUBLICATION DATA
Carter, Angela, 1940–
Saints and strangers.
(King Penguin)
Contents: The Fall River axe murders—The kiss—
Our Lady of the Massacre—[etc.]
I. Title.
[PR6053.A73S24 1987]   823'.914   87-8816
ISBN 0 14 00.8973 X

Printed in the United States of America by
R. R. Donnelley & Sons Company, Harrisonburg, Virginia
Set in Sabon

Contents

Acknowledgements

"Black Venus" was originally published in 1980 in the series, "Next Editions." "The Kiss" first appeared in *Harper's and Queen* (1977). "Overture and Incidental Music to a Midsummer Night's Dream" and "The Cabinet of Edgar Allan Poe" both first appeared in *Interzone* (1982). A version of "The Kitchen Child" was published in *Vogue* (1979) and of "Peter and the Wolf" in *Firebird I* (1982). "Our Lady of the Massacre" first appeared under a different title in the anthology, *The Saturday Night Reader* (1979). In the United States, "The Cabinet of Edgar Allan Poe" appeared first in *Free Spirits: Annals of the Insurgent Imagination*, later in *The Dark Light Years* and "Black Venus" appeared in *Formation*.

The Fall River Axe Murders

*Lizzie Borden with an axe
Gave her father forty whacks
When she saw what she had done
She gave her mother forty one.*
Children's rhyme

Early in the morning of the fourth of August, 1892, in the city of Fall River, Massachusetts.

Hot, hot, hot. Even though it is early in the morning, well before the factory whistle issues its peremptory summons from the dark, satanic mills to which the city owes its present pre-eminence in the cotton trade, the white, furious sun already shimmers and quivers high in the still air.

Nobody could call the New England summer a lovable thing; the inhabitants of New England have never made friends with it. More than the heat, it is the humidity that makes it scarcely tolerable. The weather clings, like a low fever you cannot shake off. The Indians who first lived here had the sense to take off their buckskins as soon as things hotted up and sit, thereafter, up to their necks in ponds. This behaviour is no longer permissible in the "City of Spindles."

However, as in most latitudes with similar summers, everything slows down in these dog days. The blinds are drawn, the shutters closed; all indoors becomes drowsy penumbra in which to nap away the worst heat of the day, and when they venture out again in the refreshed evening, they put on thin clothes loose enough to let cool air circulate refreshingly between the muslin and the skin, so that warm weather, as nature intended, is a sweet, sensual, horizontal thing.

But the descendants of the industrious, self-mortifying saints who imported the Protestant ethic wholesale into a land intended for the siesta are proud of flying in the face of nature. The moment the factory whistle blares—bustle! bustle! bustle! And the stern fathers of Fall River will step briskly forth into the furnace, well wrapped up in flannel underclothes, linen shirts, vests and coats and trousers of good, thick wool, and—final touch—a strangulatory neck tie, as if discomfort were next to godliness.

On this burning morning when, after breakfast and the performance of a few household duties, Lizzie Borden will murder her parents, she will, on rising, don a simple cotton frock that, if worn by itself, might be right for the weather. But, underneath, has gone a long, starched cotton petticoat; another starched cotton petticoat, a short one; long drawers; woolen stockings; a chemise; and a whalebone corset that takes her viscera in an unkind hand and squeezes them very tightly.

There is also a heavy linen napkin strapped between her legs because she is menstruating.

In all these clothes, out of sorts and nauseous as she is, in this dementing heat, her belly in a vice, she will heat up a flatiron on a stove and press handkerchiefs with the heated iron until it is time for her to go down to the cellar wood-pile to collect the hatchet with which our imagination— "Lizzie Borden with an axe"—always equips her, just as we always visualise Saint Catherine rolling along her wheel, the emblem of her passion.

Soon, in just as many clothes as Miss Lizzie wears, if less fine, Bridget, the servant girl, will slop kerosene on a sheet of last night's newspaper, rumpled up around a stick or two of kindling. When the fire settles down, she will cook breakfast. The fire will keep her company as she washes up afterward, when the mercury pauses briefly at eighty-five before recommencing its giddy ascent upwards.

In a blue serge suit one look at which would be enough to bring you out in prickly heat, old Andrew Borden will perambulate the perspiring town truffling for money like a pig until he will return home mid-morning when he will find his death, unannounced, waiting for him.

In a mean house on Second Street in the smoky city of Fall River, five living creatures are sleeping in the still, warm early morning. They comprise two old men and three women. The first old man owns all the women by either marriage, birth, or contract. His house is narrow as a coffin and that was how he made his fortune—he used to be an undertaker but he has recently branched out in several directions and all his branches bear fruit of the most fiscally gratifying kind.

But you would never think, to look at his house, that he is a successful and prosperous man. His house is cramped, comfortless—"unpretentious," you might say, if you were sycophantic, while Second Street itself saw better days some time ago. The Borden house—see "Andrew J. Borden" in flowing script on the brass plate next to the door—stands by itself with a few scant feet of yard on either side. On the left is a stable, out of use since he sold the horse. In the back lot grow a few pear trees, laden at this season.

On this particular morning, as luck would have it, only one of the two Borden girls sleep in their father's house. Emma Lenora, his oldest daughter, has taken herself off to nearby New Bedford for a few days, to catch the ocean breeze.

Few of their social class stay in sweltering Fall River in the sweating months of June, July, and August. But then, few of their social class live on Second Street, in the low part of town where heat gathers like fog. Lizzie was invited away, too, to a summer house by the sea to join a merry band of girls but, as if on purpose to mortify her flesh, as if important business kept her in the exhausted town, as if a wicked fairy spelled her on Second Street, she did not go.

The other old man is some kind of kin of Borden's. He doesn't belong, here; he is a chance bystander, he is irrelevant.

Write him out of the script.

Even though his presence in the doomed house is historically unimpeachable, the colouring of this domestic apocalypse must be crude and the design profoundly simplified for the maximum emblematic effect.

Write John Vinnicum Morse out of the script.

One old man and three of his women sleep in the house on Second Street. These women comprise his second wife, his youngest daughter, and his servant girl.

The City Hall clock whirs and sputters the prolegomena to the first stroke of six and Bridget's alarm clock gives a sympathetic skip and click as the minute hand stutters on the hour; back the little hammer jerks, about to hit the bell on top of her clock, but Bridget's damp eyelids do not shudder with premonition as she lies in her sticking flannel nightgown under one thin sheet on an iron bedstead, lies on her back, as the good nuns taught her in her Irish girlhood, in case she dies during the night, to make less trouble for the one who lays her out.

She is a good girl, on the whole, although her temper is sometimes uncertain and then she will talk back to the missus, sometimes, and will be forced to confess the sin of impatience to the priest. Overcome by heat and nausea—everyone in the house is going to wake up sick today—she will return to this little bed later on in the morning to snatch a few moments' rest. Fateful forty winks! While she indulges in them, the massacre takes place.

A rosary of brown glass beads, a cardboard-backed colour print of the Virgin bought from a Portuguese shop, a flyblown photograph of her solemn mother in Donegal—these lie or are propped on the mantelpiece that, however sharp the Massachusetts winter, has never seen a lit stick. A banged tin trunk at the foot of the bed holds all Bridget's worldly goods.

There is a stiff chair beside the bed with, upon it, a candlestick, matches, the alarm clock that resounds the room with a dyadic, metallic clang for it is a joke between Bridget and her mistress that the girl could sleep through anything, *anything,* and so she needs the alarm clock as well as all the factory whistles that are just about to blast off, just this very second about to blast off. . . .

A splintered pine washstand holds the jug and bowl she never uses; she isn't going to lug water all the way up to the third floor just to wipe herself down, is she? Not when there's water enough in the kitchen, where, in the sink, all will clean their teeth this morning.

Old Borden sees no necessity for baths. He does not believe in total immersion. To lose his natural oils would be to rob his body. Since he does not approve of baths, it goes without saying they do not maintain a bathroom.

A frameless square of mirror reflects in corrugated waves a cracked, dusty soap dish containing a quantity of black metal hair pins.

On bright rectangles of paper blinds move the beautiful shadows of the pear trees.

Although Bridget left the door open a crack in forlorn hopes of coaxing a draught into the room, all the spent heat of the previous day has packed itself tightly into her attic. A dandruff of spent whitewash flakes from the ceiling where a fly drearily whines.

Bridget's lopsided shoes stand together on a hand-braided rug of aged rags. The dress she wears for Mass on Sundays hangs from the hook on the back of the door. The calico dress she will wear for the morning's chores is folded up on the trunk where she left it last night, along with soiled underthings that will do another day.

The house is thickly redolent of sleep, that sweetish smell. Still, all still; in all the house nothing moves except the droning fly and the stillness on the staircase crushes him, he falls still. Stillness pressing against the blinds, stillness, mortal stillness in the room below, where Master and Mistress share the matrimonial bed.

Were the drapes open or the lamp lit, one could better observe the differences between this room and the austerity of the maid's room. Here is a carpet splashed with vigorous flowers even if the carpet is of the cheap and cheerful variety; there are mauve, ochre, and cerise flowers on the wallpaper, even though the wallpaper was old when the Bordens arrived in the house. A dresser with another distorting mirror; no mirror in this house does not take your face and twist it out of shape for you. On the dresser, a runner embroidered with forget-me-nots; on the runner, a bone comb missing three teeth and lightly threaded with grey hairs, a hairbrush backed with ebonised wood, and a number of lace mats underneath small china boxes holding safety pins, hairnets, et cetera. The little hairpiece that Mrs Borden attaches to her balding scalp for daytime wear is curled up like a dead squirrel.

But of Borden's male occupation of this room there is no trace because he has a dressing-room of his own, through *that* door, on the left. . . .

What about the other door, the one next to it?

It leads to the back stairs.

And that yet other door, partially concealed behind the head of the heavy mahogany bed?

If it were not kept securely locked, it would take you into Miss Lizzie's room.

It is a peculiarity of the house, that the rooms are full of doors and—a further peculiarity—all these doors are always kept locked. A house full of locked doors that open only into other rooms with other locked doors. Upstairs and downstairs, all the rooms lead in and out of one another like a maze in a bad dream. It is a house without passages. There is no part of the house that has not been marked out as some inmate's personal territory; it is a house with no shared, no common spaces between one room and the next. It is a house of privacies sealed as close as if they had been sealed with wax on a legal document.

The only way to Emma's room is through Lizzie's. There is no way out of Emma's room. It is a dead end.

The Bordens' custom of locking all the doors, inside and outside, dates from a time, a few years ago, shortly before Bridget came to work for them, when the house was burgled. A person unknown came in through the side door while Borden and his wife had taken one of their rare trips out together. He had loaded her into a trap and set out for a farm they owned outside town, a surprise visit to ensure his tenant, a dour Swede, was not bilking him. The girls stayed at home in their rooms, napping on their beds or repairing ripped hems, or sewing loose buttons more securely, or writing letters, or contemplating acts of charity among the deserving poor, or staring vacantly into space.

I can't imagine what else they might do.

What the girls do when they are on their own is unimaginable to me. Emma is even more of a mystery than Lizzie because we know less about her. She is a blank space. She has no life. The door from her room leads only into the room of her younger sister.

"Girls" is, of course, a courtesy term. Emma is well into her forties, Lizzie, her thirties, but they did not marry and so live on in their father's house, where they remain in a fictive, protracted childhood, "girls" for good.

In this city of working women, the most visible sign of the status of the Borden girls is that they toil not. "Clickety clack, clickety clack, You've got to work till it breaks your back!" the looms sing to the girls they lured here, the girls fresh from Lancashire, the dark-browed Portuguese, the French Canadian farmers' daughters, the up-country girls, the song whose rhythms now govern the movements of their dexterous fingers. But the Borden girls are deaf to it.

Strange, that endless confinement of these perpetual "girls" who do not labour in the mean house of the rich man. Strange, marginal life that those who lived it believed to be the very printing on the page, to be just exactly why the book was printed in the first place, to be the way all decent folks lived.

While the master and mistress were away and the girls asleep or otherwise occupied, some person or persons unknown tiptoed up the back stairs to the matrimonial bedroom and pocketed Mrs Borden's gold watch and chain, the collar necklace and silver bangle of her remote childhood, and a roll of dollar bills old Borden kept under his clean union suits in the third drawer of the bureau on the left. The intruder attempted to force the lock of the safe, that featureless block of black iron like a slaughtering block or an altar sitting squarely next to the bed on Old Borden's side, but it would have taken a crowbar to adequately penetrate the safe and the intruder tackled it with a pair of nail scissors that were lying handy on the dresser, so *that* didn't come off.

Then the intruder pissed and shitted on the cover of the Bordens' bed, knocked the clutter of this and that on the dresser to the floor, smashing a brace of green and violet porcelain parakeets into a thousand fragments in the process, swept into Old Borden's dressing room, there to maliciously assault his funeral coat as it hung in the moth-balled dark of his closet with the selfsame nail scissors that had been used on the safe, which now split in two and were abandoned on the closet floor, retired to the kitchen, smashed the flour crock and the treacle crock, and then scrawled an obscenity or two on the parlour window with the cake of soap that lived beside the scullery sink.

What a mess! Lizzie stared with vague surprise at the parlor window; she heard the soft bang of the open screen door, swinging idly, although there was no breeze. What was she doing, standing clad only in her corset in the middle of the sitting room? How had she got there? Had she crept down when she heard the screen door rattle? She did not know. She could not remember.

It was well known in polite circles in Fall River that Lizzie suffered from occasional "peculiar spells," as the idiom of the place and time called odd lapses of behaviour, unexpected, involuntary trances, moments of disconnection—those times when the mind misses a beat.

The Indians cursed the land with madness and death.

Even on the sunniest days, you could not say the landscape smiled; the ragged woodland, the ocean beaten out of steel. Not much, here, to cheer the heart, and all beneath the avenging light. The Indians stuck a few flints of their hard-cornered language onto the map, those names like meals of stones—Massachusetts, Pawtuxet, Woonsocket. And there are certain fruits of the region, such as the corn, especially those strange ears of crimson corn—some of the kernels are black, they dry out and rattle, you cannot eat them but people, nowadays, like to hang them on their doors for decoration in the fall—that strange, archaic-looking corn; and various squashes, the long-necked, pale yellow butternut, and the squat, whorled acorn squash, pine-green with a splatter of orange on one flank—squash and pumpkin that look and feel like votive objects carved from wood; you must boil them for hours to make them soft and then they taste flat, insipid, alien. These fruits have the ineradicable somberness of the aborigines.

From puberty, she had been troubled by these curious lapses of consciousness that often, though not always, came at the time of her menses; at these times, everyday things appeared to her with a piercing, appalling clarity that rendered them mysterious beyond words, so that the harsh, serrated leaves knocking against the window were those of a tree whose name she did not know in which sat birds whose names were not yet invented, whirring, clicking, and chucking like no birds known before, while a sputtering radiance emanated from everything. All the familiar things, at those times, seemed to her not only unknown but also unknowable, always unknowable.

So the strangers must have felt after they watched the boat that brought them slide away from them over the horizon and, abandoned, turned their faces inland towards the wilderness with the anguish of the new-born confronted with infinite space.

Time opened in two; suddenly she was not continuous any more.

Dull headaches announced the approaches of these trances, from which she returned as from an electric elsewhere. She would quiver with exhaustion; her sister would bathe her temples with a handkerchief moistened with eau de cologne, she lying on her bedroom sofa.

She had no words with which to describe the over-clarity with which she had seen the everyday things around her, even had she wished to do so. She kept the knowledge she was discontinuous to herself—or, rather, she steadfastly ignored the knowledge that she was discrete because the notion had no meaning to her, or, perhaps, too much meaning for her to assimilate since she believed that either a person was, or else was not. But don't think because she believed this that she believed it *in so many words* . . . she believed it in the same way that she believed she lived in Fall River, Massachusetts, and in the same way that she believed the second Mrs Borden had married her father for his money. She did not believe she believed in these things; she thought she *knew* them for a fact, just as she knew the Portuguese were pigs and God was the Father Almighty.

Therefore these intermittent lapses in day-to-day consciousness, in which she was and was not at the same time, were unaccountable in every way and she did not dare to think of them once she came back to herself. So she remained a stranger to herself.

A trap rattled by in the street outside. A child burst out crying in a house across the way. Lizzie experienced the departure of vision as though it were the clearing of a haze.

"Help! We have been burgled! Help!"

I cannot tell you what effect the burglary had on Borden. It utterly disconcerted him; he was a man stunned. It violated him, even. He was a man raped. It took away his hitherto unshakeable confidence in the integrity inherent in things.

The family broke its habitual silence with one another in order to discuss the burglary, it moved them so. They blamed it on the Portuguese, mostly, but sometimes on the Canucks. If their outrage remained constant and did not diminish with time, the focus of it varied according to their moods, although they always pointed the finger of suspicion at the strangers who lived in the dark ramparts of the company housing a few stinking blocks away. They did not always suspect the dark strangers exclusively; sometimes they thought the culprit might very well have been one of the mill hands fresh from saucy Lancashire across the ocean who did the deed, for a slum landlord has few friends among the criminal classes. Sometimes Lizzie voiced the notion that the lugubrious and monosyllabic Swede out on Old Borden's bit of property at Swansea might have been harbouring a grudge against her father for some reason and, when the old man gruffly reminded her the Swede had the unshakeable alibi of Borden's own presence at the time of the offence, she would fall silent and fix upon the middle distance the large, accusing, blue stare of her pale eyes.

The possibility of a poltergeist occurred to Mrs Borden, although she does not know the word; she knows, however, that her younger step-daughter could make the plates jump out of sheer spite, if she wanted to. But the old man adores his daughter. Perhaps it is then, after the shock of the burglary, that he decided she needed a change of scene, a dose of sea air, a long voyage.

The only defence against further depredation was to lock everything and then lock it again, to lock and relock everything and then lock it up once more for luck.

After the burglary, the front door and the side door were always locked three times if one of the inhabitants of the house left it for just so long as to go into the yard and pick up a basket of fallen pears when pears were in season, or if the maid went out to hang a bit of washing or Old Borden, after supper, took a piss under a tree.

From this time dated the custom of locking all the bedroom doors on the inside when one was on the inside oneself or on the outside when one was on the outside. Old Borden locked his bedroom door in the morning, when he left it, and put the key in sight of all on the kitchen shelf.

The burglary awakened Old Borden to the evanescent nature of private property. He thereafter undertook an orgy of investment. He would forthwith invest his surplus in good brick and mortar for who can make away with an office block?

A number of leases fell in simultaneously at just this time on a certain street in the downtown area of the city and Borden snapped them up. When he owned the block, he pulled it down. He planned the Borden building, an edifice of shops and offices, dark red brick, deep tan stone, with cast iron detail, from whence, in perpetuity, he might reap a fine harvest of unsaleable rents, and this monument, like that of Ozymandias, would long survive him—indeed, still stands, foursquare and handsome, the Andrew Borden Building on South Main Street.

Not bad for a fish peddler's son, eh? To turn yourself into a solid piece of real estate?

For, although "Borden" is an ancient name in New England and the Borden clan between them owned the better part of Fall River, our Borden, Old Borden, these Bordens, did not spring from a wealthy branch of the family. There were Bordens and Bordens and he was the son of a man who sold fresh fish in a wicker basket from house to house to house. Old Borden's parsimony was bred of poverty but learned to thrive best on prosperity for thrift has a different meaning for the poor; they get no joy of it, it is stark necessity to them. But a penniless miser is a contradiction in terms.

Morose and gaunt, this self-made man is one of few pleasures. His vocation is capital accumulation.

What is his hobby?

Why, grinding the faces of the poor.

First, Andrew Borden was an undertaker and death, recognising an accomplice, did well by him. In the city of spindles, few made old bones; the little children who laboured in the mills died with especial frequency. When he was an undertaker, no!—it was not true he cut the feet of corpses to fit into a job lot of coffins bought cheap as Civil War surplus! That was a rumour put about by his enemies!

With the profits from his coffins, he bought up a tenement or two and made fresh profit from the living. He bought shares in the mills. Then he invested in a brace of banks, so that now he makes a profit on money itself, which is the purest form of profit of all.

Foreclosures and evictions are meat and drink to him. He loves nothing better than a little usury. He is halfway on the road to his first million.

At night, to save the kerosene, he sits in lampless dark. He waters the pear trees with his own urine; waste not, want not. As soon as the daily newspapers are done with, he rips them into squares and stores them in the cellar privy so that they can wipe their arses with them. He mourns the loss of the good organic waste that goes down the privy. He would like to charge the very cockroaches in the kitchen rent. And yet he has not grown fat on all this; the pure flame of his passion has melted off his flesh, his skin sticks to his bones out of sheer parsimony. Perhaps it is from his first profession that he has acquired his bearing, for he walks with the stately dignity of a hearse.

To watch Old Borden bearing down the street toward you was to be filled with an instinctual respect for mortality, whose gaunt ambassador he seemed to be. And it made you think, too, what a triumph over nature it was when we rose up to walk on two legs instead of four, in the first place! For he held himself upright with such ponderous assertion it was a perpetual reminder to all who witnessed his progress how it is not *natural* to be upright, that it is a triumph of the will over gravity, in itself a transcendence of the spirit over matter.

His spine is like an iron rod, forged, not born, impossible to imagine that spine of Old Borden's curled up in the womb in the big C-shape of the fetus; he walks as if his legs had joints at neither knee nor ankle so that his feet strike at the trembling earth like a bailiff pounding a door with an iron bar.

He has a white, chin-strap beard, old-fashioned already in those days. His lips are so thin it looks as if he'd gnawed them off. He is at peace with his god for he has used his talents as the Good Book says he should.

Yet do not think he has no soft spot. Like Old Lear, like Old Goriot, his heart—and, more than that, his cheque-book—is putty in his youngest daughter's hands. On his pinky—you cannot see it, it lies under the covers—he wears a gold ring, not a wedding ring but a high school ring, a singular trinket for fabulously misanthropic miser. His youngest daughter gave it to him when she left school and asked him to wear it, always, and so he always does, and will wear it to the grave.

He sleeps fully dressed in a flannel nightshirt over his long-sleeved underwear, and a flannel nightcap, and his back is turned toward his wife of thirty years, as is hers to his.

They are Mr and Mrs Jack Spratt in person, he, tall and gaunt as a hanging judge and she, such a spreading, round little doughball. He is a miser, while she—she is a glutton, a solitary eater, most innocent of vices and yet the shadow or parodic vice of his, for he would like to eat up all the world, or, failing that, since fate has not spread him a sufficiently large table for his ambitions—he is a mute, inglorious Napoleon, he does not know what he might have done because he never had the opportunity—since he has not access to the entire world, he would like to gobble up the city of Fall River. But she, well, she just gently, continuously stuffs herself, doesn't she; she's always nibbling away at something, at the cud, perhaps.

Not that she gets much pleasure from it, either; no gourmet, she, forever meditating the exquisite difference between a mayonnaise sharpened with a few drops of Orleans vinegar or one pointed up with a squeeze of fresh lemon juice. No. Abby never aspired so high, nor would she ever think to do so even if she had the option; she is satisfied to stick to simple gluttony and she eschews all overtones of the sensuality of consumption. Since she relishes not one single mouthful of the food she eats, she knows her ceaseless gluttony is no transgression.

Here they lie in bed together, living embodiments of two of the Seven Deadly Sins, but he knows his avarice is no offence because he never spends any money and she knows she is not greedy because the grub she shovels down gives her dyspepsia. Gives her dyspepsia and worse; in those days, great-grandmother's days, summer and salmonella came in together.

Refrigeration is, perhaps, the only unmitigated blessing that the Age of Technology has brought us, a blessing that has brought no bane in tow, a wholly positive good that can be welcomed without reluctance or qualification. The white-enamelled refrigerator is the genius of every home, the friendly chill of whose breath has banished summer sickness and the runs for good! How often, nowadays, in summer does your milk turn into a sour jelly, or your butter separate itself out into the liquid fat and the corrupt-smelling whey? When did you last see the waxy clusters of the seed-pearl eggs of the blowfly materialise disgustingly on the left-over joint? Perhaps, perfect child of the Frigidaire, you've known none of all this! In those days, however, you took your life in your hands each time you picked up your knife and fork.

On the Saturday preceding the murders, for dinner, at twelve, the Bordens had a big joint of roast mutton, hot. Bridget cooked it. They must have had potatoes with it. Mashed, probably. With flour gravy. I don't know if they had greens or not. The documents don't say. But we know the main items of the Bordens' diet during their last week living because the police thoroughly investigated the rumour that the parents had been poisoned before they had been butchered and so the week's dolorous bill of fare was recorded in full.

On Saturday, they had more mutton, cold, for supper. They ate their roast on Saturdays because they were Sabbatarians and did not believe work should be done on Sundays, so Bridget had Sunday off, to go to church.

Because Bridget had Sundays off, they ate more cold mutton for Sunday dinner, with bread and butter, I dare say, and pickles, perhaps.

On Monday, they had mutton for midday dinner. I don't know how

Bridget fixed the mutton; perhaps she warmed it up in left-over gravy, to make a change from having it cold. They had mutton for breakfast on Tuesday, too. It must have been a veritably gargantuan joint of mutton—or did the fault lie with Old Borden; did he carve thin as paper money and lay the slice on the plate with as much disinclination as if he'd been paying back a loan, so the eaters felt he grudged each bite?

There was an ice-box of the old-fashioned, wooden kind, the doors of which must be kept tightly shut at all times or else the ice melts and everything inside goes rotten. Every morning, Bridget put out the pan for the ice-man and filled up the dripping ice-compartment.

In this ice-box, she lodged the remains of the mutton.

In and out of the ice-box went the joint of mutton.

On Tuesday, it was time for a change. They had sword-fish for midday dinner. Bridget bought the thick steaks of sword-fish in a fish-market that smelled like a brothel after a busy night. She put the sword-fish in the ice-box until it was time to grill it. Then the left-over sword-fish went back into the ice-box until supper time, when she warmed it up again. That was the night they vomited again and again.

Bridget kept back the knuckle from the leg of mutton in order to make broth; perhaps the broth was comforting to an upset stomach and perhaps not. They had the broth for Wednesday dinner, followed by mutton, again. Was that warmed over, too? On Wednesday, they had cold mutton for supper, again.

There is nothing quite like cold mutton. The sinewy, grey, lean meat amidst the veined lumps of congealed fat, varicosed with clotted blood; it must be the sheep's Pyrrhic vengeance on the carnivore! Considering that which lay upon her plate, Mrs Borden's habitual gluttony takes on almost an heroic quality. Undeterred by the vileness of the table, still she pigs valiantly away while the girls look on, push their own plates away, wince to see the grease on her chin.

Oh, how she loves to eat! She is Mrs Jack Spratt in person, round as a ball, fat as butter . . . the heavy fare of New England, the chowders, the cornmeal puddings, the boiled dinners, have shaped her, and continue to shape her.

See her rub her bread round her plate. "Is there a little more gravy, Bridget, just to finish up my bread?" She pours cold gravy, lumpy with flour, onto her plate, so much gravy she's forced, in the end, to cut herself just another little corner of bread with which to finish up the gravy.

The sisters think, she eats and eats and eats; she eats everything, she will eat up every single thing, crunch up the plate from which she eats when no more gravy is forthcoming, munch through the greenbacks in father's safe for a salad, for dessert she will polish off the gingerbread house in which they live.

If the old woman thought to deceive them as to her true nature by affecting to confine her voracity only to comestibles, Lizzie knew better; her guzzling stepmother's appetite terrified and appalled her, for it was the only thing within the straight and narrow Borden home that was not kept within confinement.

There had never been any conversation at table; that was not their style. Their stiff lips would part to request the salt, the bread, the butter, yes; but, apart from that, only the raucous squawk of knife on plate and private sounds of chewing and swallowing amplified and publicised and rendered over-intimate, obscene, by the unutterable silence of the narrow dining room. A strip of flypaper hung from a nail over the table, bearing upon it a mourning band of dead flies. A stopped clock of black marble, shaped like a Greek mausoleum, stood on the sideboard, becalmed. Father sat at the head of the table and shaved the meat. Mrs Borden sat at the foot and ate it.

"I won't eat with her; I won't," said Lizzie. "I refuse to sit at the trough with that sow."

After this little explosion of ill temper, Bridget served the meal twice, once for Mr and Mrs Borden, then kept all warm and brought it out again for Lizzie and Emma, since Emma knew it was her duty to take the part of her little sister, her little dearest, the tender and difficult one. After this interruption, calm returned to the household; calm continued to dominate the household.

Saturday, Sunday, Monday, Tuesday, Wednesday. In and out of the ice-box went the slowly dwindling leg of mutton until Thursday dinner was cancelled because corpses and not places were laid out on the table as if the eaters had become the meal.

Back to back they lie. You could rest a sword in the space between the old man and his wife, between the old man's backbone, the only rigid thing he ever offered her, and her soft, warm, enormous bum. Her flannel nightdress is cut on the same lines as his nightshirt except for the limp flannel frill around the neck. She weighs two hundred pounds. She is five feet nothing tall. The bed sags on her side. It is the bed in which his first wife died.

Last night, they dosed themselves with castor oil, due to the indisposition that kept them both awake and vomiting the whole night before that; the copious results of their purges brim the chamberpots beneath the bed.

Their purges flailed them. Their faces show up decomposing green in the dim, curtained room, in which the air is too thick for flies to move.

The youngest daughter dreams behind the locked door.

She threw back the top sheet and her window is wide open but there is no breeze outside this morning to deliciously shiver the screen. Bright sun floods the blinds so that the linen-coloured light shows us how Lizzie has gone to bed as for a levée in a pretty, ruffled nightdress of starched white muslin with ribbons of pastel pink satin threaded through the eyelets of the lace, for is it not the "naughty nineties" everywhere but dour Fall River? Don't the gilded steamships of the Fall River Line signify all the squandered luxury of the Gilded Age within their mahogany and chandeliered interiors? Elsewhere, it is the Belle Epoque. In New York, Paris, London, champagne corks pop and women fall backwards in a crisp meringue of petticoats for fun and profit but not in Fall River. Oh, no. So, in the immutable privacy of her bedroom, for her own delight, Lizzie puts on a rich girl's pretty nightdress, although she lives in a mean house, because she is a rich girl, too.

But she is plain.

The hem of her nightdress is rucked up above her knees because she is a restless sleeper. Her light, dry, reddish hair, crackling with static, slipping loose from the nighttime plait, crisps and stutters over the square pillow at which she clutches as she sprawls on her stomach, having rested her cheek on the starched pillowcase for coolness's sake at some earlier hour.

Lizzie was not an affectionate diminutive but the name with which she had been christened. Since she would always be known as "Lizzie," so her father reasoned, why burden her with the effete and fancy prolongation of "Elizabeth"? A miser in everything, he even cropped off half her name before he gave it to her. So "Lizzie" it was, stark and unadorned, and she is a motherless child, orphaned at two years old, poor thing.

Now she is two-and-thirty and yet the memory of that mother whom she cannot remember remains an abiding source of grief: "If mother had lived, everything would have been different."

How? Why? Different in what way? She wouldn't have been able to answer that, lost in a nostalgia for lost affection. Yet how could she have been loved better than by her sister, Emma, who lavished the pent-up treasures of a New England spinster's heart upon the little thing? Different, perhaps, because her natural mother, the first Mrs Borden, subject as she was to fits of sudden, wild, inexplicable rage, might have taken the hatchet to Old Borden on her own account? But Lizzie *loves* her father. All are agreed on that. Lizzie adores the adoring father who, after her mother died, took to himself another wife.

Her bare feet twitch a little, like those of a dog dreaming of rabbits. Her sleep is thin and unsatisfying, full of vague terrors and indeterminate menaces to which she cannot put a name or form once she is awake. Sleep opens within her a disorderly house. But all she knows is, she sleeps badly, and this last, stifling night has been troubled, too, by vague nausea and the gripes of her female pain; her room is harsh with the metallic smell of menstrual blood.

Yesterday evening she slipped out of the house to visit a woman friend. Lizzie was agitated; she kept picking nervously at the shirring on the front of her dress.

"I am afraid ... that somebody ... will *do* something," said Lizzie.

"Mrs Borden ..." and here Lizzie lowered her voice and her eyes looked everywhere in the room except at Miss Russell ... "Mrs Borden—oh! will you ever believe? Mrs Borden thinks somebody is trying to *poison* us!"

She used to call her stepmother "mother," as duty bade, but after a quarrel about money after her father deeded half a slum property to her stepmother five years before, Lizzie always, with cool scrupulosity, spoke of "Mrs Borden" when she was forced to speak of her and called her "Mrs Borden" to her face, too.

"Last night, Mrs Borden and poor father were so sick! I heard them, through the wall. And, as for me, I haven't felt myself all day, I have felt so strange. So very ... strange."

Miss Russell hastened to discover an explanation within reason; she was embarrassed to mention the "peculiar spells." Everyone knew there was nothing odd about the Borden girls. It was Lizzie's difficult time of the month, too; her friend could tell by a certain haggard, glazed look on Lizzie's face when it was happening. Yet her gentility forbade her to mention that.

"Something you ate? It must have been something you have eaten. What was yesterday's supper?" solicitously enquired Miss Russell.

"Warmed-over swordfish. We had it hot for dinner though I could not take much. Then Bridget heated up the left-overs for supper but, again, for myself, I could only get down a forkful. Mrs Borden ate up the remains and scoured her plate with her bread. She smacked her lips but then was sick all night." (Note of smugness, here.)

"Oh, Lizzie! In all this heat, this dreadful heat! Twice-cooked fish! You know how quickly fish goes off in this heat! Bridget should have known better than to give you twice-cooked fish!"

"There have been threats," Lizzie pursued remorselessly, keeping her eyes on her nervous fingertips. "So many people, you understand, dislike father."

This cannot be denied. Miss Russell politely remained mute.

"Mrs Borden was so very sick she called the doctor in and Father was abusive toward the doctor and shouted at him and told him he would not pay a doctor's bills whilst we had our own good castor oil in the house. He shouted at the doctor and all the neighbours heard and I was so ashamed. There is a man, you see . . ." and here she ducked her head, while her short, pale eyelashes beat on her cheekbones . . . "such a man, a *dark* man, Portuguese, Italian, I've seen him outside the house at odd, at unexpected hours, early in the morning, late at night, whenever I cannot sleep in this dreadful heat if I raise the blind and peep out, there I see him in the shadows of the pear trees, in the yard . . . perhaps he puts poison in the milk, in the mornings, after the milk-man fills his can.

"Perhaps he poisons the ice, when the ice-man comes."

"How long has he been haunting you?" asked Miss Russell, properly dismayed.

"Since . . . the burglary," said Lizzie and suddenly looked Miss Russell full in the face with a kind of triumph. How large her eyes were, prominent, yet veiled. And her well-manicured fingers went on pecking away at the front of her dress as if she were trying to unpick the shirring.

Miss Russell knew, she just *knew,* this dark man was a figment of Lizzie's imagination. All in a rush, she lost patience with the girl; dark men standing outside her bedroom window, indeed! Yet she was kind and cast about for ways to reassure her.

"But Bridget is up and about when the milk-man and the ice-man call and the whole street is busy and bustling, too; who would dare to put poison in either milk or ice-bucket while half of Second Street looks on? Oh, Lizzie, it is the dreadful summer, the heat, the intolerable heat that's put us all out of sorts, makes us fractious and nervous, makes us sick. So easy to imagine things in this terrible weather, that taints the food and sows worms in the mind. . . . I thought you'd planned to go away, Lizzie, to the ocean. Didn't you plan to take a little holiday, by the sea? Oh, do go! Sea air would blow away all these silly fancies!"

Lizzie neither nods nor shakes her head but continues to worry at her shirring. For does she not have important business in Fall River? Only that morning, had she not been down to the drug-store to try to buy some prussic acid? But how can she tell kind Miss Russell she is gripped by an imperious need to stay in Fall River and murder her parents?

Had all that talk of poison in the vomiting house put her in mind of poison? She went to the drug-store on the corner of Main Street in order to buy prussic acid but nobody would sell it to her so she came home empty-handed. When she asked the corner pharmacist only that morning for a little prussic acid to kill the moth in her seal-skin cape, the man looked at her oddly. "Moth don't breed in seal-skin," he opined. The autopsy will reveal no trace of poison in the stomachs of either parent. She did not try to poison them; she only had it in mind to poison them.

"And this dark man," she pursued to the unwilling Miss Russell, "oh! I have seen the moon glint upon his knife!"

When she wakes up, she can never remember her dreams; she only remembers she slept badly.

Hers is a pleasant room of not ungenerous dimensions, seeing the house is so very small. Besides the bed and the dresser, there is a sofa and a desk; it is her bedroom and also her sitting room and her office, too, for the desk is stacked with account books of the various charitable organisations with which she occupies her ample spare time. The Fruit and Flower Mission, under whose auspices she visits the indigent old in the hospital with gifts; the Women's Christian Temperance Union, for whom she extracts signatures for petitions against the Demon Drink; Christian Endeavour, whatever that is—this is the golden age of good works and she flings herself into committees with a vengeance. What would the daughters of the rich do with themselves if the poor ceased to exist?

Then there is the Newsboys Thanksgiving Dinner Fund; and the Horsetrough Association; and the Chinese Conversion Association—no class nor kind is safe from her merciless charity.

She used to teach a Sunday school class of little Chinese children but they did not like her; they teased her, they played an unpleasant trick on her, one Sunday afternoon they put a dead dog inside her desk, a trick of which one would have thought the Chinese were incapable because they are so impassive and did not even giggle when she shrieked.

First, she shrieked; then she caught hold of the shoulder of the little Chinese boy sitting at the end of the front row—the nearest child she could get at—and started in on hitting him but then the class instantly abandoned its impassivity and let out such a racket the superintendent came before much damage was done. The children were severely punished. They were forbidden to come to Sunday school again.

Bureau; dressing-table; closet; bed; sofa. She spends her days in this room, moving between each of these dull items of furniture in a circumscribed, undeviating, planetary round. She loves her privacy, she loves her room, she locks herself up in it all day. A shelf contains a book or two: *Heroes of the Mission Field, The Romance of Trade*. On the walls, framed photographs of high school friends, sentimentally inscribed, with, tucked inside one frame, a picture postcard showing a black kitten peeking through a horseshoe. A watercolour of a Cape Cod seascape executed with poignant amateur incompetence. A monochrome photograph of two works of art, a Della Robbia madonna and the Mona Lisa; these she bought in the Uffizi and the Louvre, respectively, when she went to Europe.

Europe!

For don't you remember What Katy Did Next? The storybook heroine took the steamship to smoky old London, to elegant, fascinating Paris, to sunny, antique Rome and Florence; the storybook heroine sees Europe reveal itself before her like an interesting series of magic lantern slides on a gigantic screen. All is present and all unreal. The Tower of London; click. Notre Dame; click. The Sistine Chapel; click. Then the lights go out and she is in the dark again.

Of this journey she retained only the most circumspect of souvenirs, that madonna, that Mona Lisa, reproductions of objects of art consecrated by a universal approval of taste. If she came back with a bag full of memories stamped "Never to be Forgotten," she put the bag away under the bed on which she had dreamed of the world before she set out to see it and on which, at home again, she continued to dream, the dream having been transformed not into lived experience but into memory, which is only another kind of dreaming.

Wistfully: "When I was in Florence . . ."

But then, with pleasure, she corrects herself: "When *we* were in Florence . . ."

Because a good deal, in fact, most of the gratification the trip gave her came from having set out from Fall River with a select group of the daughters of respectable and affluent mill owners. Once away from Second Street, she was able to move comfortably in the segment of Fall River society to which she belonged by right of old name and new money but from which, when she was at home, her father's plentiful personal eccentricities excluded her. Sharing bedrooms, sharing staterooms, sharing berths, the girls travelled together in a genteel gaggle that bore its doom already upon it for they were the girls who would not marry, now, and any pleasure they might have obtained from the variety and excitement of the trip was spoiled in advance by the knowledge they were eating up what might have been their own wedding-cake, using up what should have been, if they'd had any luck, their marriage settlements.

All girls pushing thirty, privileged to go out and look at the world before they resigned themselves to the thin condition of New England spinsterhood; but it was a case of look, don't touch. They knew they must not get their hands dirtied or their dresses crushed by the world, while their affectionate companionship en route had a certain steadfast, determined quality about it as they bravely made the best of the second-best.

It was a sour tour, in some ways, and it was a round trip; it ended at the sour place from which it had set out. Home, again, the narrow house, the rooms all locked like those in Bluebeard's Castle, and the fat, white stepmother whom nobody loves sitting in the middle of the spider web; she has not budged a single inch while Lizzie was away but she has grown fatter.

This stepmother oppressed her like a spell. Lizzie will immediately correct the judge at her trial: "She is not my mother, sir; she is my stepmother: my mother died when I was a child." But Old Borden brought his new bride home when his younger girl was five!

Another mystery—how the Bordens contrived to live together for twenty, nearly thirty years without generating amongst themselves a single scrap of the grumbling, irritable, everyday affection without which proximity becomes intolerable; yet their life cannot have been truly intolerable, because they lived it for so long. They bore it. They did not rub along together, somehow; they rubbed each other up the wrong way all the time, and yet they lived in each others' pockets.

Correction: they lived in Old Borden's pocket and all they had in common was the contents of that pocket.

The days open their cramped spaces into other cramped spaces and old furniture and never anything to look forward to, nothing. Empty days. Oppressive afternoons. Nights stalled in calm. Empty days.

When Old Borden dug in his pocket to shell out for Lizzie's trip to Europe, the eye of God on the pyramid blinked to see daylight but no extravagance is too excessive for the miser's younger daughter who is the wild card in this house and, it seems, can have anything she wants, play ducks and drakes with her father's silver dollars if it so pleases her. He pays all her dressmakers' bills on the dot and how she loves to dress up fine! In her unacknowledged, atrocious solitude, she has become addicted to dandyism. He gives her each week in pin money the same as the cook gets for wages and Lizzie gives that which she does not spend on personal adornment to the deserving poor.

He would give his Lizzie anything, anything in the world that lives under the green sign of the dollar.

She would like a pet, a kitten or a puppy; she loves small animals and birds, too, poor, helpless things. She piles high the bird-table all winter. She used to keep some white pouter pigeons in the disused stable, the kind that look like shuttlecocks and go "vroo croo" soft as a cloud.

Surviving photographs of Lizzie Borden show a face it is difficult to look at as if you knew nothing about her; coming events cast their shadow across her face, or else you see the shadows these events have cast—something terrible, something ominous in this face with its jutting, rectangular jaw and those mad eyes of the New England saints, eyes that belong to a person who does not listen . . . fanatic's eyes, you might say, if you knew nothing about her. If you were sorting through a box of old photographs in a junk shop and came across this particular sepia, faded face above the choker collars of the eighteen-nineties, you might murmur when you saw her: "Oh, what big eyes you have!" as Red Riding Hood said to the wolf, but then you might not even pause to pick her out and look at her more closely, for hers is not, in itself, a striking face.

But as soon as the face has a name, once you recognise her, when you know who she is and what it was she did, the face becomes as if of one possessed, and now it haunts you, you look at it again and again, it secretes mystery.

This woman, with her jaw of a concentration camp attendant; and such eyes . . .

In her old age, she wore pince-nez and truly with the years the mad light has departed from those eyes or else is deflected by her glasses—if, indeed, it *was* a mad light, in the first place, for don't we all conceal somewhere photographs of ourselves that make us look like crazed assassins? And, in those early photographs of her young womanhood, she herself does not look so much like a crazed assassin as somebody in extreme solitude, oblivious of that camera in whose direction she obscurely smiles, so that it would not surprise you to learn that she is blind.

There is a mirror on the dresser in which she sometimes looks at those times when time snaps in two and then she sees herself with clairvoyant eyes, as though she were another person.

"Lizzie is not herself, today."

At those times, those irremediable times, she could have raised her muzzle to an aching moon and howled.

At other times, she watches herself doing her hair and trying her clothes on. The distorting mirror reflects her with the queasy fidelity of water. She puts on dresses and then she takes them off. She looks at herself in her corset. She measures herself with the tape measure. She pulls the measure tight. She pats her hair. She tries on a hat, a little hat, a chic little straw toque. She punctures it with a hatpin. She pulls the veil down. She pulls it up. She takes the hat off. She drives the hatpin into it with a vivacious strength she did not know she possessed.

Time goes by and nothing happens.

She traces the outlines of her face with an uncertain hand as if she were thinking of unfastening the bandages on her soul but it isn't time to do that, yet; her new face isn't ready to be seen, yet.

She is a girl of Sargasso calm.

She used to keep her pigeons in the loft above the disused stable and feed them grain out of the palms of her cupped hands. She liked to feel the soft scratch of their little beaks. They murmured "vroo croo" with infinite tenderness. She changed their water every day and cleaned up their leprous messes but Old Borden took a dislike to their cooing, it got on his nerves—who'd have thought he *had* any nerves? But he invented some, they got on them, and one afternoon he took out the hatchet from the wood-pile in the cellar and chopped the pigeons' heads off.

Abby fancied the slaughtered pigeons for a pie but Bridget the servant girl put her foot down, at that; What?!? Make a pie out of Miss Lizzie's beloved turtledoves? JesusMaryandJoseph!!! she exclaimed with characteristic impetuousness; what can they be thinking of! Miss Lizzie so nervy with her funny turns and all! (The maid is the only one in the house with any sense and that's the truth of it.) Lizzie came home from the Fruit and Flowers Mission where she had been reading a tract to an old woman in a poorhouse: "God bless you, Miss Lizzie." At home all was blood and feathers.

She doesn't weep, this one, it isn't her nature, she is still waters, but, when moved, she changes colour, her face flushes, it goes dark, angry, mottled red, marbling up like the marbling on the inner covers of the family Bible. The old man loves his daughter this side of idolatry and pays for everything she wants but all the same he killed her pigeons when his wife wanted to gobble them up.

That is how she sees it. That is how she understands it. Now she cannot bear to watch her stepmother eat. Each bite the woman takes seems to go "vroo croo."

Old Borden cleaned off the hatchet and put it back in the cellar, next to the wood-pile. The red receding from her face, Lizzie went down to inspect the instrument of destruction. She picked it up and weighed it in her hand.

That was a few weeks before, at the beginning of the spring.

Her hands and feet twitch in her sleep; the nerves and muscles of this complicated mechanism won't relax, just won't relax; she is all twang, all tension; she is as taut as the strings of a wind-harp from which random currents of the air pluck out tunes that are not our tunes.

At the first stroke of the City Hall clock, the first factory hooter blares, and then, on another note, another, and another, the Metacomet Mill, the American Mill, the Mechanics Mill . . . until every mill in the entire town sings out aloud in a common anthem of summoning and the hot alleys where the factory folk live blacken with the hurrying throng, hurry! scurry! to loom, to bobbin, to spindle, to dye-shop as to places of worship, men, and women, too, and children, the street blackens, the sky darkens as the chimneys now belch forth, the clang, bang, and clatter of the mills commences.

Bridget's clock leaps and shudders on its chair, about to sound its own alarm. Their day, the Bordens's fatal day, trembles on the brink of beginning.

Outside, above, in the already burning air, see! the angel of death roosts on the roof-tree.

The Kiss

The winters in Central Asia are piercing and bleak, while the sweating, foetid summers bring cholera, dysentery and mosquitoes, but, in April, the air caresses like the touch of the inner skin of the thigh and the scent of all the flowering trees douses this city's throat-catching whiff of cesspits.

Every city has its own internal logic. Imagine a city drawn in straightforward, geometric shapes with crayons from a child's colouring box, in ochre, in white, in pale terracotta. Low, blonde terraces of houses seem to rise out of the whitish, pinkish earth as if born from it, not built out of it. There is a faint, gritty dust over everything, like the dust those pastel crayons leave on your fingers.

Against these bleached pallors, the irridescent crusts of ceramic tiles that cover the ancient mausoleums ensorcellate the eye. The throbbing blue of Islam transforms itself to green while you look at it. Beneath a bulbous dome alternately lapis lazuli and veridian, the bones of Tamburlaine, the scourge of Asia, lie in a jade tomb. We are visiting an authentically fabulous city. We are in Samarkand.

The Revolution promised the Uzbek peasant women clothes of silk and on this promise, at least, did not welch. They wear tunics of flimsy satin, pink and yellow, red and white, black and white, red, green and white, in blotched stripes of brilliant colours that dazzle like an optical illusion, and they bedeck themselves with much jewellery made of red glass.

They always seem to be frowning because they paint a thick, black line straight across their foreheads that takes their eyebrows from one side of their faces to the other without a break. They rim their eyes with kohl. They look startling. They fasten their long hair in two or three dozen whirling plaits. Young girls wear little velvet caps embroidered with metallic thread and beadwork. Older women cover their heads with a couple of scarves of flower-printed wool, one bound tight over the forehead, the other hanging loosely on to the shoulders. Nobody has worn a veil for sixty years.

They walk as purposefully as if they did not live in an imaginary city.

They do not know that they themselves and their turbanned, sheep-skin jacketted, booted menfolk are creatures as extraordinary to the foreign eye as a unicorn. They exist, in all their glittering and innocent exoticism, in direct contradiction to history. They do not know what I know about them. They do not know that this city is not the entire world. All they know of the world is this city, beautiful as an illusion, where irises grow in the gutters. In the tea-house a green parrot nudges the bars of its wicker cage.

The market has a sharp, green smell. A girl with black-barred brows sprinkles water from a glass over radishes. In this early part of the year, you can buy only last summer's dried fruit – apricots, peaches, raisins – except for a few, precious, wrinkled pomegranates, stored in sawdust through the winter and now split open on the stall to show how a wet nest of garnets remains within. A local speciality of Samarkand is salted apricot kernels, more delicious, even, than pistachios.

An old woman sells arum lilies. This morning, she came from the mountains, where wild tulips have put out flowers like blown bubbles of blood, and the wheedling turtle-doves are nesting among the rocks. This old woman dips bread into a cup of buttermilk for her lunch and eats slowly. When she has sold her lilies, she will go back to the place where they are growing.

She scarcely seems to inhabit time. Or, it is as if she were waiting for Scheherezahde to perceive a final dawn had come and, the last tale of all concluded, fall silent. Then, the lily-seller might vanish.

A goat is nibbling wild jasmine among the ruins of the mosque that was built by the beautiful wife of Tamburlaine.

Tamburlaine's wife started to build this mosque for him as a surprise, while he was away at the wars, but when she got word of his imminent return, one arch still remained unfinished. She went directly to the architect and begged him to hurry but the architect told her that he would complete the work in time only if she gave him a kiss. One kiss, one single kiss.

Tamburlaine's wife was not only very beautiful and very virtuous but also very clever. She went to the market, bought a basket of eggs, boiled them hard and stained them a dozen different colours. She called the architect to the palace, showed him the basket and told him to choose any egg he liked and eat it. He took a red egg. What does it taste like? Like an egg. Eat another.

He took a green egg.

What does *that* taste like? Like the red egg. Try again.

He ate a purple egg.

One egg tastes just the same as any other egg, if they are fresh, he said.

There you are! she said. Each of these eggs looks different to the rest but they all taste the same. So you may kiss any one of my serving women that you like but you must leave me alone.

Very well, said the architect. But soon he came back to her and this time he was carrying a tray with three bowls on it, and you would have thought the bowls were all full of water.

Drink from each of these bowls, he said.

She took a drink from the first bowl, then from the second; but how she coughed and spluttered when she took a mouthful from the third bowl, because it contained, not water, but vodka.

This vodka and that water both look alike but each tastes quite different, he said. And it is the same with love.

Then Tamburlaine's wife kissed the architect on the mouth. He went back to the mosque and finished the arch the same day that victorious Tamburlaine rode into Samarkand with his army and banners and his cages full of captive kings. But when Tamburlaine went to visit his wife, she turned away from him because no woman will return to the harem after she has tasted vodka. Tamburlaine beat her with a knout until she told him she had kissed the architect and then he sent his executioners hotfoot to the mosque.

The executioners saw the architect standing on top of the arch and ran up the stairs with their knives drawn but when he heard them coming he grew wings and flew away to Persia.

This is a story in simple, geometric shapes and the bold colours of a child's box of crayons. This Tamburlaine's wife of the story would have painted a black stripe laterally across her forehead and done up her hair in a dozen, dozen tiny plaits, like any other Uzbek woman. She would have bought red and white radishes from the market for her husband's dinner. After she ran away from him perhaps she made her living in the market. Perhaps she sold lilies there.

Our Lady of the Massacre

———————

My name is neither here nor there since I used several in the Old World that I may not speak of now; then there is my, as it were, *wilderness* name, that now I never speak of; and, now, what I call myself in *this* place, therefore my name is no clue as to my person nor my life as to my nature. But I first saw light in the county of *Lancashire* in *Old England*, in the Year of Our Lord 16—, my father a poor farm servant, and me mam and he both died of plague when I was a little thing so me and me brothers and sisters left living were put on the parish and what became of them I do not know, but, as for me, I could do a bit of sewing and keep a place clean so when I were nine or ten year of age they set me up as a maid of all work to an old woman that lived in our parish.

This old woman, or *lady*, rather, never married and was, as I found out, of the Roman faith, though she kept *that* to herself, and once a good deal richer than she had become. Besides, her father, wanting a son and getting nowt but she, taught her Latin, Greek and a bit of Hebrew and left her a great telescope with which she used to view the heavens from her roof though her sight was too bad to make out much but what she did not see, she made up, for she said she had poor sight for the things of *this* world but clear sight into the one to come. She often let me have a squint at the stars, too, for I was her only companion and she learned me my letters, as you can see, and would have taught me all she knew herself, had she not, as soon as I come to her, cast my *horoscope* for me, her father having left her the charts and zodiacal instruments. And, having done so, told me I would not need the language of *Homer* at no time in all my life, but a little conversational Hebrew she *did* teach me, for reasons as follows:

That the stars, whom she had consulted on behalf of her dear child, as she pleased to call me, assured her that I should take a long voyage over the Ocean to the *New World* and there bear a blessed babe whose fathers' fathers never sailed in Noah's Ark. And, from her reading, which had worn her eyes out, she had concluded that those 'red children of the wilderness' could be none other than the Lost Tribe of Israel, so 'shalom', she taught me, besides the words for 'love' and 'hunger', and much else that I have forgotten, so that I could talk to my husband when I met him. And if I had not been a steady girl, she would have turned my head with all her nonsense for she would have it that the stars foretold I should grow up to be nowt less than Our Lady of the Red Men.

For, she says, that country far beyond the sea is named *Virginia*, after the virgin mother of God Almighty, and its rivers flow directly from Eden so, when the natives are converted to the true religion – 'which task I charge you with, child,' and she gives me a mouthful of Ave Marias – when that shall be accomplished, why, the whole world will end and the dead rise up out of their coffins and all go to heaven that deserve it and my little babby sit smiling over everything with a gold crown on his head. Then she'd babble away in Latin and cross herself. But I never told nobody about her *Roman* ways nor about her star-gazing, either, for if they hadn't hanged her for a heretic, they'd have hanged her for a witch, poor creature.

One day the old lass lies down and never gets up again and her cousins come and shift all the goods with a penn'orth of value to 'em but they could find no place for me in their house so I must shift for meself.

I take it into my head to go to *London*, where I persuade myself I can make my fortune, and I walk the highway, sleeping in barns and hedges, for I was hardy, and makes good time – five days. When I gets to London, I stole my first penny loaf, to keep me from starving, which led directly to my undoing, a gentleman that spies me slip the loaf into my pocket, instead of raising the hue and cry, follows me into the street, takes my arm, inquires: whether it be want or inclination that makes me take it. I flares up at that: Want, sir! says I and he says, such a pretty young 'Lancashire milkmaid' as I was should not want for nothing while he had breath in his body and so flattered and coaxed me that I went with him to a room with a bed in it in a public house where he was well known. When he finds I'd never done the thing before, he weeps; beats his breast for shame for debauching me; gives me five golden sovereigns, the most money that ever I saw until then; and departs for, so he says, the church, to pray forgiveness, which is the last that I saw of him. So I went on the common with my first fall, which was a fortunate one, and the 'Lancashire milkmaid' was soon in a fair way of trade as the 'Lancashire whore.'

Now, had I been content with honest whoring, no doubt I should be dressed in silk riding my coach in Cheapside still and never eat the bitter bread of exile. But you could say that, when I clapped my eye on his coin, I was as if struck with love and though want made a thief of me, first, it was avarice perfected me in the art and whoring was my 'cover' for it since my customers, blinded as they were with lust and often fuddled with liquor, were easier to pluck, living, than geese, dead.

It was a gold watch out of the bosom of a city alderman that took me to Newgate for I quarrelled with my landlady over my rent and she took his complaint of me to the magistrate out of spite. So, just as my old Lancashire mistress said, I sailed the Ocean to *Virginia* but I went in a convict transport. They burned my hand, to brand me, as they use convicts, and sold me to work my sentence in the plantation for seven year, after which they said I should be a free woman again.

My master took a liking to me, for I was not yet aged above seventeen, and he had me out of the tobacco fields into his kitchen. But the overseer did not like it, that I should get the taste of his whip no more, and pestered me unmercifully that, since I had been a whore in Cheapside, I should not play the honest maid with him in *Virginia*. Coming at me alone in the house, my master having gone to church, it being Sunday morning, this overseer thrusts one hand in my bosom and the other up my skirt, says I shall have it whether I wants it or no. I picked up the big carving knife and whacks off both his ears, first one, then t'other. What a sight! blood enough for pig-sticking; he roars, he curses, I runs out into the garden with the knife in my hand, it dripping.

Seeing me in such a fluster, the gardener coming up with a basket of vegetables cries: 'What's this, Sal?'

'Well,' says I, 'the overseer just now tried to board me and I've had the ears off him and would it had been his pillocks, too.'

The gardener, being a good-natured kind of *Negro* man and a slave, hisself, and hisself tickled once too often by the overseer's whip, cannot forbear to laugh but says to me: 'Then you must be off into the wilderness, Sal, and cast your fate to the tender mercies of the savage Indian. For this is a hanging matter.'

He gives me his handkerchief with his bit of dinner in it and a tinder-box he had about him, which I stow away in my apron pocket, and I show the plantation a clean pair of heels, I can tell you, adding to my list of crimes that most heinous: escape from bondage.

I am a good walker as you may judge from my trudge from Lancashire to London and by the time night comes on and I sit down to eat the gardener's bit of bread and bacon there were fifteen odd miles between myself and the plantation and rough going, too, for my master had cleared land from the forest to grow his tobacco. My plan is, to walk until I gets to where the English have no dominion, for I have heard the Spaniards and the French are on this coast, as well, and there, I thought, I'd ply my trade amongst strangers, for a whore needs nowt but her skin to set up business.

You must know I had no knowledge of *geography* and thought, from *Virginia* to *Florida* but ten or twelve days march, at the most, for I knew it was very far and could think of no distance further than that, for the great vastness of the *Americas* was then unknown to me. As for the Indians, I thought, well! if I can keep off that overseer with my knife, I'd be more than a match for them, if I should meet them, so slept sound under the sky, took a bearing by the sun in the morning and went on.

I had clean water out of the streams and it was the season of berries so I made my breakfast off a bit of fruit but my guts began to rumble by dinner-time and I cast my eye about for more solid fodder. Seeing the brakes full of small beasts and birds unknown to me, I thought: 'How can I go hungry if I use my wits!' So I tied my shoestrings together to make a little snare and trapped a small, brown, furry thing of the rabbit kind, but earless, and slit its throat, skinned it, toasted it on the end of my carving-knife over a fire I made with the blessed tinder-box the gardener give me. So all I wanted was salt and a bit of bread.

After I eat my dinner, I saw how the oak trees were full of acorns at this season and thought that I might grind up those acorns between two flat stones, with a bit of effort, and so get a kind of flour, as had been done at home in times of want. I reasoned how I could mix this flour to dough with water. Then I could bake the dough in cakes in the ashes of my fire and have bread with my meat. And, if I wanted fish on a Friday, as was my Lancashire lady's custom, I could tickle the trout with which the stream abounded, which is a trick every country girl knows and not unlike picking a pocket. Also, it seemed to me, if I dried the mulberries in the sun, they would eat sweet for months. When I got so far in planning my diet, I thought: why, I can get along here very well in the woods on me own for a while even if I must eat meat without salt!

For, I thought, I have steel and fire and the climate is temperate, the land fruitful; this earthly paradise surely will provide for me! I can build a shelter out of branches and bide my time until the fuss over the lop-eared overseer dies down, then make my way South in my own good time. Besides, to tell the truth, my nostrils were too full of the stink of humanity to relish a quick return to the world in some bordello in *Florida*. But I thought that I should travel on a little more, for safety's sake, into the deep wilderness, so that no hunting party might find me and return me to the noose. Of which I had a very powerful fear and, I may tell you, more dread of the *white man*, which I knew, than of the *red man*, who was at that time unknown to me.

So I walked on another day, taking my living from the country easily enough; then one day more and never heard a voice but the birds' whistle; but the day after that I heard a woman singing and saw one of the savage tribe in a clearing and thought to kill her, before she killed me, but then I saw she had no weapon but was picking herbs and putting them in a fine basket. So I steps back to hide myself from her lest she be some Indian servant of a planter, although I do think that I walk, now, where no person of my country ever trod before. But she hears the leaves move and sees me and jumps as if she'd seen a ghost so that she knocks over her basket and her herbs spill out.

I never think twice about it but step across to pick up the spilled herbs for her as if I was back in Cheapside and run to help some fruit-seller that overturns her basket of apples.

This woman sees the brand on my hand and grunts to herself, as though she knows the meaning of it and will not fear me for it, or, rather, does not fear me because of it, but, all the same, does not like the look of me. She holds back from me though she takes her basket from me again as if to leave me in the forest. But I am struck by her looks, she is a handsome woman, not red but wondrous brown, and it came into my mind to open my bodice, show her my breasts, that, though I had the whiter skin, I could give suck as well as she and she reached out and touched my bosom.

She was a woman of about the middle age dressed in nowt but a buckskin skirt and she grunted when she saw my stays – for I still wore my *English apparel*, though it was ragged – and motioned me, as I thought, that whalebone was not the fashion among the Indian nation. So off go my stays and I throws them into a bush and breathes easier for it. Then she asks me, by signs, to give her the big knife I'd stuck in my apron.

'Now I'm for it!' I thinks but hands it over and she smiles, though not much, for these savages are not half so free with their feelings as we are, and says a word I take to mean: 'Knife'. I say it after her, pointing to it, but she shakes her head and runs her finger down the blade, so I say, after her: 'Sharp'. Or, a word you might put into English as: acute. And that was the first word of the *Algonkian* language that ever I spoke, though not the last, by any means. Then, seeing this old woman with a shape, not, as I can see, marked by child-bearing, and remembering the Virgin Queen my missus taught me of, I try her out with: 'Shalom'. Which she politely repeats after me but I can tell it means nowt to her.

She motions me: shall I go with her? I think the overseer will never come to look for me among the *red men*! So I goes with her to the Indian town and in this way, no other, was I 'taken' by 'em although the Minister would have it otherwise, that they took me with violence, against my will, haling me by the hair, and if he wishes to believe it, then let 'im.

Their clean, pretty town was built within a low wood fence or stockade, the houses built of birchbark set in gardens with vines with pumpkins on 'em and the cooking of their meat savouring the air, as it was about dinner-time. They were cooking what they call *succotash*, a great pot on an open fire and a naked savage squatting before it, calm as you please, fanning the flames with a birchbark fan. The town was surrounded by tidy fields of tobacco and corn and a river near. But no kind of beast did I see, nor cows nor horses nor chickens, for they keep none. She takes me to her own lodge, where she lives by herself on account of her business, and gives me water to wash in and a bunch of feathers to dry myself, so that I was much refreshed.

I had heard these Indians were mortal dragons, accustomed to eat the flesh of dead men, but the pretty little naked children playing with their dollies in the dust, oh! never could such little ducks be reared on cannibal meat! And my Indian 'mother', as I soon called her, assured me that though their cousins to the North roasted the thighs of their captives and ceremoniously partook thereof, it was, as you might say, a *sacramental meal*, to honour the departed by devouring him; and I have often disputed with the Minister on this point, that the Iroquois dinner is but the *Mass* in a state of nature. And the Minister will say, either: that I lived so long with Satan that I grew accustomed to his ways, or, that the Romish *Mass* is but the Iroquois feast in britches.

As for me, all I ever eat among the Indians was fish, game or fowl, boiled or broiled, besides corn cooked in various ways, beans, squash in season and etc. and this such a healthy diet that it is very rare to see a sick body amongst them and never did I see there any either shaking with palsy or suffering toothache or with sore eyes or crooked with age.

The weather being warm, at first I blushed to see the nakedness of the savages, for the men were accustomed to go clad in nowt but breech-clouts at that season and the women with only a rag about 'em. But soon I thought nothing of it and exchanged my petticoat for the buckskin one my mother give me and she give me a necklace, too, of the beads they carve from shells, for she said she had no daughter of her own to pet until the woods sent her this one, whom she was thankful to the English for giving away.

There was no end of the kindness of this woman to me and I lived in her cabin with her, for she had no husband, since she was, as it were, the *midwife* of the tribe and all her time taken up with seeing to women in their labour. And it was to make potions to ease the labour pains and the pains of the women in their courses that she was picking herbs in the woods when I first saw her.

How do they live, these so-called demi-devils? The men among them have an easy life, spend all their time in leisure and idleness, except when they are hunting or fighting their enemies, since all their tribes are constantly at war with one another, and with the English, too; and the *werowance*, as they call him, he is not the chief, or ruler of the village, although the English do say that he is so, but, rather, he is the man who goes the first in battle, so he is commonly more courageous a man than the English generals who direct their soldiers from the back.

As for me, I stayed with my Indian mother in her hut and learned from her Indian manners, such as sitting on my knees on the ground to my meat that was spread on a mat before me because they have no furniture. I learned how to cure and dress robes out of buckskin, beaver and other skins, and to embroider them with shell and feathers. I had a housewife with me in my apron pocket and my mother was very pleased with the steel needles, likewise with the tinder-box, which she was glad to get, while my carving-knife she thought a wonderfully convenient thing, they having no notion of working metal although the women make good pots out of the river clay and bake 'em in an open fire very cleverly while you never see a beard on any man, since they contrive to shave themselves all over quite close with razors of stone.

And I should say that one or two *guns* they *did* have, for a little while before I arrived among 'em, there came a Scotsman, swapping guns and liquor in return for dressed robes and, as for the effects of the liquor, I shall say nowt about it except it sends 'em mad, but, as for the guns, they had soon learned to use them.

The harvest coming on, they gathered up their corn, a very poor, small sort of corn, to my way of thinking, the heads just *that* much bigger than my thumb, and we dug holes in the ground six or seven feet deep and what of the corn we did not eat we dried and stored away under the earth. But the digging was a great labour for they have no shovels or spades except what they steal from the English so we made shift with sticks or the shoulder-bones of deer. And if I have one quarrel with my tribe, it is that the men will have nothing to do with this *agriculture*, although it is heavy work, but go fishing in the creek or chase deer or engage in dances and such silly performances as they say will make the corn grow.

But my mother said: 'There is no harm in it and it keeps the men *out of the way*.'

By the time the weather turned, I was rattling away in the Indian language as if I'd been born to it, though not a word of Hebrew did it contain so I think my old Lancashire lady was mistaken that they are the Lost Tribe of Israel and, as to converting them to the *true religion*, I was so busy with one thing and another that it never entered my head. As for my *pale face*, by the end of the harvest it was brown as any of theirs and my mother stained my light hair for me with some darkish dye so they grew accustomed to my presence among them and at six months end you would have thought she whom I called my 'mother' was my own natural mother and I was Indian born and bred, except my blue eyes remained a marvel.

But for all the bonds of affection between us, I might still have thought of journeying on to *Florida* as the weather grew colder, such is the power of custom and habit, had I not cast my eye on a *brave* of that tribe who had no woman for himself and he cast his eye on me but never a word he says, it seems all along he intends to do the *right thing* by me, so it was my mother said to me at last: 'That *Tall Hickory* you know of would like you for a wife.' *Tall Hickory* being what his name signified in English, and as common a kind of name amongst 'em as James or Matthew might be in Lancashire.

And now it comes to it, I wept, for he was a fine man.

'How can I be that good man's wife, mother, for I was a bad woman in my own country.'

'A bad woman?' she says. 'What's this?'

So I told her what I did to earn my living on Cheapside; and how I was a thief by natural vocation. As for my whoring, she was very much surprised to hear that English men would trouble to pay for such a thing as I had to sell, for the Indians exchange it free or not at all, and, as for my virginity being gone, she laughs and says: 'If you were no good, nobody would have had you.' But she grieves over my thievery until at last she says to me: 'Well, child, would you steal away a bowl or *wampun belt* or robe from out of my hut and keep it yourself and deny it to me?'

'How could I do that, mother,' says I. 'If I should need anything, I may use it and give it to you again as you do with our needles and the tinder-box and the knife. And so it is with such-a-one and such-a-one –' naming our neighbours. 'And to tell the truth, there is nowt in all the village excites my old passion of avarice, while as for my dinner, if I need it, I may have a share in any cooking pot in the Indian country, for that is the custom. So neither *desire* nor *want* can make a thief of me, here.'

'Then you are a good woman in spite of yourself among the Indians and so I think you will remain,' she says. 'Why not marry the young fellow?'

Now, certain men of the village, such as the *general*, and the *priest*, as I might call him, seeing he dealt with religion, had not one wife but three or four to till their fields for them and I did not like that, I would be the only one in my husband's lodge, a fancy of the old life that I could not lose. And she puzzles over that, although she herself was never any man's husband, having, so she tells me with a wink, not much liking for the sex and much fondness for her own.

'As for ourselves, we are too seemly and decent a folk for the matter of matrimony to come between a woman and her friends!' she says. 'The more wives a man has, the better company for them, the more knees to dandle the children on and the more corn they can plant so the better they all live together.'

But still I said, I would be his *only wife* or never marry him.

'Listen, my dear,' she said. 'Do you not love me?'

'Indeed I do,' I says, 'with all my heart.'

'Then if your sweetheart should offer to marry us both, would you love me the less for it?'

But I ducked my head and forbore to answer that, for fear she should ask my beau to take her, too, along with me, since I was so struck with him I could not think that any woman, however set in her ways, would not have him if she got half the chance. Then she gives me a clout on the buttocks and cries out: 'Now, child, see what a wretched thing this *jealousy* is, that it can set a daughter against her own mother!'

But she relents to see me cry for shame and says, she is too old and stubborn to think of marriage and, besides, my young man is so taken with me that he will marry me on my own terms in the English fashion. For they are taught to love their wives and let them have their way no matter how many of them they marry and, if I wanted the toil of tilling a patch of corn with nowt but my own two hands, then he would not interfere with that.

We were married about the time they were planting the corn, which they celebrate with a good deal of singing and dancing although it is we squaws who break our backs setting the seeds. The season of the anniversary of my arrival in the town passed, winter comes again and by the spring I was well on the way to bringing him a little *brave*. It was marvellous to see the tenderness of my husband's bearing towards me when the sun grew hot and made me sweat, weary, heavy, peevish, so that I often swore I wished meself in England again; but he bore with all.

Now, at this time, the *general* of our village held counsel how all the tribes of this part of the territory should settle their differences and join together in a great army to drive the English off back to where they come from while some of the others said, they should, instead, make treaties with the English against those other tribes who were their *natural enemies* and so get more guns from the English.

But I sent word by my husband – the women did not go to the counsels but were accustomed to let their husbands give their messages – I sent word by him that it would take all the tribes of all the continent to drive away the English, and then the English would only go away to come again in double numbers, so eager were they to 'plant the colony' with me and such poor devils as I had been. So I told them straight they must make a grand, warlike, well-armed confederacy amongst all the Indian nations and never trust a word the English said, for the English would all be thieves if they could, and I was living proof of it, who only left off thieving when there was nothing to steal.

But they took no notice of me, and could not agree about the manner in which, if they should wage it, the war should be waged, whether an attack on Annestown by night, creeping on all fours like bears with bows in their mouths; or picking off the Englishmen one by one when they went hunting or out in lonely places; or meeting 'em head on, like an army. Which they fancied best, because it was most honourable, but, to my way of thinking, putting the head in the beast's mouth. While some still held that the English were their friends because they were their *enemies' enemy*. So they fell to squabbling amongst themselves and nothing came of all the talk which was a great sadness to me, for I was with child and so I wanted a quiet life.

I was scratching away with my pointed stick along the garden bean-row until the very minute the waters broke and I goes running into my mother and, an hour later, as I judge it, for they have no means of keeping exact time, she was washing the blood off my young son.

My young son we named what would be, in English, *Little Shooting Star*, and you may laugh at it, but it is a name fine men have carried. And he was strapped into his little board that he might ride on my back in his birchbark carriage and I was as pleased with him as any woman might be. Which is how the fate my old Lancashire lady foresaw for me came to pass, because my boy's father never sprang from the tribe of Shem, Ham nor Japhet, although his mother resembled more the Mary Magdalene, or repentant harlot, than Mary the Virgin, though the Minister does not hold with that stuff, being a dissenting man, and will not let me speak of it.

But it would come about that the little lad's crown must be of tears, not gold.

Now, the confederacy among the *Algonkians* breaking up, the depredations of the English upon the villages towards the South grew week by week more severe but our fierce braves held them off a while. The generals of this region held a parley as to whether all stay and defend our villages or else beat a retreat, that is, stir our stumps and pick up our traps and leave our fields and shift westwards a piece, to new pastures, after the harvest, which was at hand. But this latter they were loath to do, since to the West lay the *Rechacrians*, a very warlike tribe not easily crossed. And they sent out a *war party* to give the English a taste of their own medicine, to start off with, but I was full of fear lest my husband not come back.

He paints his face up black and red so the babby cried to see and they do go out and all come back, with blood on their axes, and several scalps of yellow hair that he hangs on the ridgepole of the roof, besides plunder of copper kettles, bullets and gunpowder. Also, alas, rum.

Yet I must say, when I first saw those English topknots, I felt nowt but pleasure though their hair was of my colour; yet the Minister says I am a good girl and God will forgive me for the sins I committed among the Indians.

As for gunpowder, *Tall Hickory*, my husband, told me, when the English first give it to the general, years back, the English told him, with much secret merriment amongst themselves, how he should bury it, like seed corn, and watch the bullets come up. And the Indians held it as a grudge ever after, to have been teased like silly children, when the English would have starved dead if the Red Men had not taught 'em how to plant corn.

Their captive they brought back lashed to the powder barrel and taunted him, how they would set their torches to a slow fuse, left him there in the middle of the village and abused him in their drunkenness for they were devils when they'd got a bit of drink inside 'em, I must admit it.

'Now, my dear,' says my husband, who was stone-cold sober because he'd a mortal terror of the edge of my tongue. 'I must ask you to talk to this fellow in your own language, that we might know if his fellow-countrymen will at last remember certain pledges and treaties formerly made between us or do indeed mean to drive us into the arms of the *Rechacrians*, with whom we are on no friendly terms, so it will be the worse for us, trapped between the two.'

At first I would not do it because I felt some pity for this Englishman, they were very stern with their captives and made a cruel festival out of this one, what with the drink and all. Then I recall how I saw this fellow riding his high horse along the dock at Annestown when the convicts were unloaded in chains from the holds of the ships and all pity left me.

When he hears my English, 'Praise the Lord!' he cries, and tells me straightaway how I must give over my tribes to the whites in the name of God, the King of England, and a free pardon thrown in when he sees my brand. But I shows him the babby and he calls me all kind of foul names, to whore among the heathen, so I shoves a sharp stick in his belly to teach him manners. He squawks at that but will say nothing of the soldiers or where they might be but only: that the damned seed shall be driven from the land. Then they took him off the barrel, for they did not want to waste good gunpowder on him, and hoist him up over the fire. Soon he was dead.

When I went through his pockets, they were stuffed full of coin and all the children come to play ducks and drakes with gold pieces on the river. But his gold watch I wound up and give my husband in remembrance of the one I robbed the alderman of.

'What's this?' he says in his innocence. Just then it rang the hours of twelve, it being noon, and he screeches out, drops it, it breaks apart, the wheels and springs scatter on the ground, and my husband, poor, superstitious savage that he was for all he was the best man in the world, my husband fell a-shaking and a-trembling and said the watch was 'bad medicine' and boded ill.

So he went off and got drunk with the rest. I go through the papers in the gentleman's pockets and find out we've put an end to the governor of all Virginia and I tells 'em so, full of misgiving at it, but they was all so far gone in liquor no sense to be had out of any of 'em until they slept it off but just before sun-up next day the soldiers came on horseback.

They burned the ripe cornfields and set light to the stockade so it burned and our lodge burned when the powder went up so I saw the massacre bright as day. They put a bullet through my husband's head, he on his feet and all bewildered, I got him out of the lodge when I first heard the fire crackle but he was a big man, couldn't miss him. And the poor drunk, sleepy savages all mown down. I got the baby in my arms and went and hid in the bird-scare in the cornfield, which was a platform on legs with a hide over it, and so escaped.

But the soldiers caught hold of my mother as she was running to the river with her hair on fire and she shouts to me, seeing me fleeing: 'You unkind daughter!' For she thought I was hastening to cast my lot in with the English, which was not so, by any means. Then they violated her, then they slit her throat. So all over quickly, by daybreak nowt left but ashes, corpses, the widow mourning her dead children, soldiers leaning on their guns well pleased with their night's work and the courageous manner in which they had revenged the governor.

The babby bust out crying. One of these brutes, hearing him, came beating among the scorched corn and pushes at the bird-scare, knocks it down so I fell out, flat on my back, the baby tumbles out of my arms and cracks his head open on a stone, sets up a terrible shrieking, even the hardest heart would have run directly to him. But this soldier puts his knee on my belly, unfastens his britches intending to rape me, he'd need the strength of ten to hold me down but all at once leaves off his horrid fumbling, amazed.

'Captain!' he says. 'Look here! Here's a squaw with blue eyes, such as I've never seen before!'

He takes a good handful of my hair and hales me to where the captain of these good soldiers is washing his bloody hands in a basin of water cool as you please while his men pick over the *wampun* and the robes for trophies of war. He asks me, what is my name and whether I speak English; then Dutch; then French; and tries me in Spanish but I will say nothing except, in the Algonkian language: 'I am the widow of *Tall Hickory*.' But he cannot understand that.

They found out I was not indeed a woman of the Indian blood at last by a trick for one of 'em fetched my baby from where they'd left him bawling in the cornfield and showed him his knife, making as if he would stick the sharp blade into my little one.

'Thou shalt not!' I cried out while the others held me back from him or I should have torn out his eyes with my bare hands. How they laughed, when the squaw with feathers in her hair shouted out in broad Lancashire. Then the captain sees my burned hand and calls me a 'runaway' and says there will be a price on my head over and above the bounty on the Indians. And teases me, how they will brand my cheek with 'R' for 'runaway' when we gets to Annestown so I cannot whore among the Indians no more, nor amongst nobody else. But all I want is the loan of his handkerchief, dipped in water, to wipe the cut on the babby's forehead and this he's kind enough to give me, at last.

When I got my babby back and put him to nurse, for he was hungry, then I went along with the soldiers, since I had no choice, my mother and my husband dead and, truth to tell, my spirit broken. And what squaws were left living, that I used to call 'sister', trailed along behind us, for the soldiers wanted women and the women wanted bread and not one brave left living in that part of the New World that now you might call a 'fair garden blasted of folk'. And the river watering this earthly paradise running blood.

The squaws blamed me, how I had brought bad luck on them and cruelly repaid their kindness to me. But, as for me, my grief is mixed with fear over the memory of the overseer I had the ears off of, that all this will end in the *downward drop*, once I am back where justice is.

We gets to a place with a few houses and they had just finished building a church and: 'Here is a morsel plucked from Satan,' says the one that widowed me to the Minister, who tells me to thank God that I have been rescued from the savage and beg the Good Lord's forgiveness for straying from His ways. Taking my cue from this, I fall to my knees, for I see that repentance is the fashion in these parts and the more of it I show, the better it will be for me. And when they ask my name, I give 'em the name of my old Lancashire lady, which was Mary, and stick by it, so I live on as if I were her ghost, and all her prophecies come true, except it turns out I was Our Lady of the Massacre and I do think my *half-breed* child will bear the mark of *Cain*, for the scar above his left eye never fades.

The Minister's wife come out of the kitchen with an old gown of hers and tells me to cover up my breasts, for shame, but the child cries and will not be pacified. Yet she is decent, and the Minister, also, as their acts now prove for they would not let the soldiers take me to Annestown with them but offered the captain a good sum of money to leave me with them, for the sake of my innocent baby. The captain hums and haws, the Minister adds another guinea, the *fine soldier* pockets the gold and all ride off and the Minister would give my child some Bible name, Isaac or Ishmael or some such name. 'Hasn't he got a good enough name already?' says I. But the Minister says: '*Little Shooting Star* is no name for a Christian,' and a baptized Christian my boy must be if his soul may be admitted to the congregation of the blessed though the poor thing will never find his daddy there. And when shall these dead rise up and be avenged? But, as for me, I will not call him by the name the Minister gave him; nor do I talk to him in any but the Indian language when nobody else is there.

After a while, the tale comes how, two years or more before, the Indians came by stealth to a plantation to the north, murdered an overseer and stole away a bonded servant girl. The gardener saw them drag her off by her yellow hair. I think to meself, how the gardener must have settled a score on his own account, good luck to him, and if they choose to think I was forced into captivity, then they have my leave to do so, if it makes them happy, as long as they leave me be. Which, because the Minister has a powerful desire to save my soul, and his wife fond of the little one, having none of her own, they do, for they've paid out good money to keep us from the law. And don't I earn my keep, do all the rough work, carry water, hew wood.

So I scrubbed the Minister's floor, cooked the dinner, washed the clothes and for all the Minister swears they've come to build the *City of God* in the *New World*, I was the same skivvy as I'd been in Lancashire and no openings for a whore in the *Community of the Saints*, either, if I could have found in my heart the least desire to take up my old trade again. But that I could not; the Indians had damned me for a *good woman* once and for all.

By and by the missus comes to me and says: 'You are still a young woman, Mary, and Jabez Mather says he will have you for a wife since his own died of the flux but he will not take the child so I shall keep it.' But *she* will never have my little lad for her son, nor will I have Jabez Mather for my husband, nor any man living, but sit and weep by the waters of Babylon.

Peter and the Wolf

At length the grandeur of the mountains becomes monotonous; with familiarity, the landscape ceases to provoke awe and wonder and the traveller sees the alps with the indifferent eye of those who always live there. Above a certain line, no trees grow. Shadows of clouds move across the bare alps as freely as the clouds themselves move across the sky.

A girl from a village on the lower slopes left her widowed mother to marry a man who lived up in the empty places. Soon she was pregnant. In October, there was a severe storm. The old woman knew her daughter was near her time and waited for a message but none arrived. After the storm passed, the old woman went up to see for herself, taking her grown son with her because she was afraid.

From a long way off, they saw no smoke rising from the chimney. Solitude yawned round them. The open door banged backwards and forwards on its hinges. Solitude engulfed them. There were traces of wolf-dung on the floor so they knew wolves had been in the house but left the corpse of the young mother alone although of her baby nothing was left except some mess that showed it had been born. Nor was there a trace of the son-in-law but a gnawed foot in a boot.

They wrapped the dead in a quilt and took it home with them. Now it was late. The howling of the wolves mutilated the approaching silence of the night.

Winter came with icy blasts, when everyone stays indoors and stokes the fire. The old woman's son married the blacksmith's daughter and she moved in with them. The snow melted and it was spring. By the next Christmas, there was a bouncing grandson. Time passed. More children came.

When the eldest grandson, Peter, reached his seventh summer, he was old enough to go up the mountain with his father, as the men did every year, to let the goats feed on the young grass. There Peter sat in the new sunlight, plaiting the straw for baskets, until he saw the thing he had been taught most to fear advancing silently along the lea of an outcrop of rock. Then another wolf, following the first one.

If they had not been the first wolves he had ever seen, the boy would not have inspected them so closely, their plush, grey pelts, of which the hairs are tipped with white, giving them a ghostly look, as if they were on the point of dissolving at the edges; their sprightly, plumey tails; their acute, inquisitive masks.

Then Peter saw that the third wolf was a prodigy, a marvel, a naked one, going on all fours, as they did, but hairless as regards the body although hair grew around its head.

The sight of this bald wolf so fascinated him that he would have lost his flock, perhaps himself been eaten and certainly been beaten to the bone for negligence had not the goats themselves raised their heads, snuffed danger and run off, bleating and whinnying, so that the men came, firing guns, making hullabaloo, scaring the wolves away.

His father was too angry to listen to what Peter said. He cuffed Peter round the head and sent him home. His mother was feeding this year's baby. His grandmother sat at the table, shelling peas into a pot.

'There was a little girl with the wolves, granny,' said Peter. Why was he so sure it had been a little girl? Perhaps because her hair was so long, so long and lively. 'A little girl about my age, from her size,' he said.

His grandmother threw a flat pod out of the door so the chickens could peck it up.

'I saw a little girl with the wolves,' he said.

His grandmother tipped water into the pot, got up from the table and hung the pot of peas on the hook over the fire. There wasn't time, that night, but, next morning, very early, she herself took the boy back up the mountain.

'Tell your father what you told me.'

They went to look at the wolves' tracks. On a bit of dampish ground they found a print, not like that of a dog's pad, much less like that of a child's footprint, yet Peter worried and puzzled over it until he made sense of it.

'She was running on all fours with her arse stuck up in the air . . . therefore . . . she'd put all her weight on the ball of her foot, wouldn't she? And splay out her toes, see . . . like that.'

He went barefoot in summer, like all the village children; he inserted the ball of his own foot in the print, to show his father what kind of mark he would have made if he, too, always ran on all fours.

'No use for a heel, if you run that way. So she doesn't have a heel-print. Stands to reason.'

At last his father made a slow acknowledgement of Peter's powers of deduction, giving the child a veiled glance of disquiet. It was a clever child.

They soon found her. She was asleep. Her spine had grown so supple she could curl into a perfect C. She woke up when she heard them and ran, but somebody caught her with a sliding noose at the end of a rope; the noose over her head jerked tight and she fell to the ground with her eyes popping and rolling. A big, grey, angry bitch appeared out of nowhere but Peter's father blasted it to bits with his shotgun. The girl would have choked if the old woman hadn't taken her head on her lap and pulled the knot loose. The girl bit the grandmother's hand.

The girl scratched and fought until the men tied her wrists and ankles together with twine and slung her from a pole to carry her back to the village. Then she went limp. She didn't scream or shout, she didn't seem to be able to, she made only a few dull, guttural sounds in the back of her throat, and, though she did not seem to know how to cry, water trickled out of the corners of her eyes.

How burned she was by the weather! Bright brown all over; and how filthy she was! Caked with mud and dirt. And every inch of her chestnut hide was scored and scabbed with dozens of scars of sharp abrasions of rock and thorn. Her hair dragged on the ground as they carried her along; it was stuck with burrs and it was so dirty you could not see what colour it might be. She was dreadfully verminous. She stank. She was so thin that all her ribs stuck out. The fine, plump, potato-fed boy was far bigger than she, although she was a year or so older.

Solemn with curiosity, he trotted behind her. Granny stumped alongside with her bitten hand wrapped up in her apron. Once the girl was dumped on the earth floor of her grandmother's house, the boy secretly poked at her left buttock with his forefinger, out of curiosity, to see what she felt like. She felt warm but hard. She did not so much as twitch when he touched her. She had given up the struggle; she lay trussed on the floor and pretended to be dead.

Granny's house had the one large room which, in winter, they shared with the goats. As soon as it caught a whiff of her, the big tabby mouser hissed like a pricked balloon and bounded up the ladder that went to the hayloft above. Soup smoked on the fire and the table was laid. It was now about supper-time but still quite light; night comes late on the summer mountain.

'Untie her,' said the grandmother.

Her son wasn't willing at first but the old woman would not be denied, so he got the breadknife and cut the rope round the girl's ankles. All she did was kick, but when he cut the rope round her writsts, it was as if he had let a fiend loose. The onlookers ran out of the door, the rest of the family ran for the ladder to the hayloft but Granny and Peter both ran to the door, to shoot the bolt, so she could not get out.

The trapped one knocked round the room. Bang – over went the table. Crash, tinkle – the supper dishes smashed. Bang, crash, tinkle – the dresser fell forward upon the hard white shale of crockery it shed in falling. Over went the meal barrel and she coughed, she sneezed like a child sneezes, no different, and then she bounced around on fear-stiffened legs in a white cloud until the flour settled on everything like a magic powder that made everything strange. Her first frenzy over, she squatted a moment, questing with her long nose and then began to make little rushing sorties, now here, now there, snapping and yelping and tossing her bewildered head.

She never rose up on two legs; she crouched, all the time, on her hands and tiptoes, yet it was not quite like crouching, for you could see how all fours came naturally to her as though she had made a different pact with gravity than we have, and you could see, too, how strong the muscles in her thighs had grown on the mountain, how taut the twanging arches of her feet, and that indeed, she only used her heels when she sat back on her haunches. She growled; now and then she coughed out those intolerable, thick grunts of distress. All you could see of her rolling eyes were the whites, which were the bluish, glaring white of snow.

Several times, her bowels opened, apparently involuntarily. The kitchen smelled like a privy yet even her excrement was different to ours, the refuse of raw, strange, unguessable, wicked feeding, shit of a wolf.

Oh, horror!

She bumped into the hearth, knocked over the pan hanging from the hook and the spilled contents put out the fire. Hot soup scalded her forelegs. Shock of pain. Squatting on her hindquarters, holding the hurt paw dangling piteously from its wrist before her, she howled, in high, sobbing arcs.

Even the old woman, who had contracted with herself to love the child of her dead daughter, was frightened when she heard the girl howl.

Peter's heart gave a hop, a skip, so that he had a sensation of falling; he was not conscious of his own fear because he could not take his eyes off the sight of the crevice of her girl-child's sex, that was perfectly visible to him as she sat there square on the base of her spine. The night was now as dark as, at this season, it would go – which is to say, not very dark; a white thread of moon hung in the blond sky at the top of the chimney so that it was neither dark nor light indoors yet the boy could see her intimacy clearly, as if by its own phosphorescence. It exercised an absolute fascination upon him.

Her lips opened up as she howled so that she offered him, without her own intention or volition, a view of a set of Chinese boxes of whorled flesh that seemed to open one upon another into herself, drawing him into an inner, secret place in which destination perpetually receded before him, his first, devastating, vertiginous intimation of infinity.

She howled.

And went on howling until, from the mountain, first singly, then in a complex polyphony, answered at last voices in the same language.

She continued to howl, though now with a less tragic resonance.

Soon it was impossible for the occupants of the house to deny to themselves that the wolves were descending on the village in a pack.

Then she was consoled, sank down, laid her head on her forepaws so that her hair trailed in the cooling soup and so closed up her forbidden book without the least notion she had ever opened it or that it was banned. Her heavy eyelids closed on her brown, bloodshot eyes. The household gun hung on a nail over the fireplace where Peter's father had put it when he came in but when the man set his foot on the top rung of the ladder in order to come down for his weapon, the girl jumped up, snarling and showing her long yellow canines.

The howling outside was now mixed with the agitated dismay of the domestic beasts. All the other villagers were well locked up at home.

The wolves were at the door.

The boy took hold of his grandmother's uninjured hand. First the old woman would not budge but he gave her a good tug and she came to herself. The girl raised her head suspiciously but let them by. The boy pushed his grandmother up the ladder in front of him and drew it up behind them. He was full of nervous dread. He would have given anything to turn time back, so that he might have run, shouting a warning, when he first caught sight of the wolves, and never seen her.

The door shook as the wolves outside jumped up at it and the screws that held the socket of the bolt to the frame cracked, squeaked and started to give. The girl jumped up, at that, and began to make excited little sallies back and forth in front of the door. The screws tore out of the frame quite soon. The pack tumbled over one another to get inside.

Dissonance. Terror. The clamour within the house was that of all the winds of winter trapped in a box. That which they feared most, outside, was now indoors with them. The baby in the hayloft whimpered and its mother crushed it to her breast as if the wolves might snatch this one away, too; but the rescue party had arrived only in order to collect their fosterling.

They left behind a riotous stench in the house, and white tracks of flour everywhere. The broken door creaked backwards and forwards on its hinges. Black sticks of dead wood from the extinguished fire were scattered on the floor.

Peter thought the old woman would cry, now, but she seemed unmoved. When all was safe, they came down the ladder one by one and, as if released from a spell of silence, burst into excited speech except for the mute old woman and the distraught boy. Although it was well past midnight, the daughter-in-law went to the well for water to scrub the wild smell out of the house. The broken things were cleared up and thrown away. Peter's father nailed the table and the dresser back together. The neighbours came out of their houses, full of amazement; the wolves had not taken so much as a chicken from the hen-coops, not snatched even a single egg.

People brought beer into the starlight, and schnapps made from potatoes, and snacks, because the excitement had made them hungry. That terrible night ended up in one big party but the grandmother would eat or drink nothing and went to bed as soon as her house was clean.

Next day, she went to the graveyard and sat for a while beside her daughter's grave but she did not pray. Then she came home and started chopping cabbage for the evening meal but had to leave off because her bitten hand was festering.

That winter, during the leisure imposed by the snow, after his grandmother's death, Peter asked the village priest to teach him to read the Bible. The priest gladly complied; Peter was the first of his flock who had ever expressed any interest in learning to read.

The boy became very pious, so much so that his family were startled and impressed. The younger children teased him and called him 'Saint Peter' but that did not stop him sneaking off to church to pray whenever he had a spare moment. In Lent, he fasted to the bone. On Good Friday, he lashed himself. It was as if he blamed himself for the death of the old lady, as if he believed he had brought into the house the fatal infection that had taken her out of it. He was consumed by an imperious passion for atonement. Each night, he pored over his book by the flimsy candlelight, looking for a clue to grace, until his mother shooed him off to sleep.

But, as if to spite the four evangelists he nightly invoked to protect his bed, the nightmare regularly disordered his sleeps. He tossed and turned on the rustling straw pallet he shared with two little ones.

Delighted with Peter's precocious intelligence, the priest started to teach him Latin. Peter visited the priest as his duties with the herd permitted. When he was fourteen, the priest told his parents that Peter should now go to the seminary in the town in the valley where the boy would learn to become a priest himself. Rich in sons, they spared one to God, since his books and his praying made him a stranger to them. After the goats came down from the high pasture for the winter, Peter set off. It was October.

At the end of his first day's travel, he reached a river that ran from the mountain into the valley. The nights were already chilly; he lit himself a fire, prayed, ate bread and cheese his mother had packed for him and slept as well as he could. In spite of his eagerness to plunge into the white world of penance and devotion that awaited him, he was anxious and troubled for reasons he could not explain to himself.

In the first light, the light that no more than clarifies darkness like egg shells dropped in cloudy liquid, he went down to the river to drink and to wash his face. It was so still he could have been the one thing living.

Her forearms, her loins and her legs were thick with hair and the hair on her head hung round her face in such a way that you could hardly make out her features. She crouched on the other side of the river. She was lapping up water so full of mauve light that it looked as if she were drinking up the dawn as fast as it appeared yet all the same the air grew pale while he was looking at her.

Solitude and silence; all still.

She could never have acknowledged that the reflection beneath her in the river was that of herself. She did not know she had a face; she had never known she had a face and so her face itself was the mirror of a different kind of consciousness than ours is, just as her nakedness, without innocence or display, was that of our first parents, before the Fall. She was hairy as Magdalen in the wilderness and yet repentance was not within her comprehension.

Language crumbled into dust under the weight of her speechlessness.

A pair of cubs rolled out of the bushes, cuffing one another. She did not pay them any heed.

The boy began to tremble and shake. His skin prickled. He felt he had been made of snow and now might melt. He mumbled something, or sobbed.

She cocked her head at the vague, river-washed sound and the cubs heard it, too, left off tumbling and ran to burrow their scared heads in her side. But she decided, after a moment, there was no danger and lowered her muzzle, again, to the surface of the water that took hold of her hair and spread it out around her head.

When she finished her drink, she backed a few paces, shaking her wet pelt. The little cubs fastened their mouths on her dangling breasts.

Peter could not help it, he burst out crying. He had not cried since his grandmother's funeral. Tears rolled down his face and splashed on the grass. He blundered forward a few steps into the river with his arms held open, intending to cross over to the other side to join her in her marvellous and private grace, impelled by the access of an almost visionary ecstasy. But his cousin took fright at the sudden movement, wrenched her teats away from the cubs and ran off. The squeaking cubs scampered behind. She ran on hands and feet as if that were the only way to run towards the high ground, into the bright maze of the uncompleted dawn.

When the boy recovered himself, he dried his tears on his sleeve, took off his soaked boots and dried his feet and legs on the tail of his shirt. Then he ate something from his pack, he scarcely knew what, and continued on the way to the town; but what would he do at the seminary, now? For now he knew there was nothing to be afraid of.

He experienced the vertigo of freedom.

He carried his boots slung over his shoulder by the laces. They were a great burden. He debated with himself whether or not to throw them away but, when he came to a paved road, he had to put them on, although they were still damp.

The birds woke up and sang. The cool, rational sun surprised him; morning had broken on his exhilaration and the mountain now lay behind him. He looked over his shoulder and saw, how, with distance, the mountain began to acquire a flat, two-dimensional look. It was already turning into a picture of itself, into the postcard hastily bought as a souvenir of childhood at a railway station or a border post, the newspaper cutting, the snapshot he would show in strange towns, strange cities, other countries he could not, at this moment, imagine, whose names he did not yet know, places where he would say, in strange languages, 'That was where I spent my childhood. Imagine!'

He turned and stared at the mountain for a long time. He had lived in it for fourteen years but he had never seen it before as it might look to someone who had not known it as almost a part of the self, so, for the first time, he saw the primitive, vast, magnificent, barren, unkind, simplicity of the mountain. As he said goodbye to it, he saw it turn into so much scenery, into the wonderful backcloth for an old country tale, tale of a child suckled by wolves, perhaps, or of wolves nursed by a woman.

Then he determinedly set his face towards the town and tramped onwards, into a different story.

'If I look back again,' he thought with a last gasp of superstitious terror, 'I shall turn into a pillar of salt.'

The Cabinet of Edgar Allan Poe

Imagine Poe in the Republic! when he possesses none of its virtues; no Spartan, he. Each time he tilts the jug to greet the austere morning, his sober friends reluctantly concur: 'No man is safe who drinks before breakfast.' Where is the black star of melancholy? Elsewhere; not here. Here it is always morning; stern, democratic light scrubs apparitions off the streets down which his dangerous feet must go.

Perhaps . . . perhaps the black star of melancholy was hiding in the dark at the bottom of the jug all the time . . . it might be the whole thing is a little secret between the jug and himself . . .

He turns back to go and look; and the pitiless light of common day hits him full in the face like a blow from the eye of God. Struck, he reels. Where can he hide, where there are no shadows? They split the Republic in two, they halved the apple of knowledge, white light strikes the top half and leaves the rest in shadow; up here, up north, in the levelling latitudes, a man must make his own penumbra if he wants concealment because the massive, heroic light of the Republic admits of no ambiguities. Either you are a saint; or a stranger. He is a stranger, here, a gentleman up from Virginia somewhat down on his luck, and, alas, he may not invoke the Prince of Darkness (always a perfect gentleman) in his cause since, of the absolute night which is the antithesis to these days of rectitude, there is no aristocracy.

Poe staggers under the weight of the Declaration of Independence. People think he is drunk.

He *is* drunk.

The prince in exile lurches through the new-found land.

So you say he overacts? Very well; he overacts. There is a past history of histrionics in his family. His mother was, as they say, born in a trunk, grease-paint in her bloodstream, and made her first appearance on any stage in her ninth summer in a hiss-the-villain melodrama entitled *Mysteries of the Castle*. On she skipped to sing a ballad clad in the pretty rags of a ballet gypsy.

It was the evening of the eighteenth century.

At this hour, this very hour, far away in Paris, France, in the appalling dungeons of the Bastille, old Sade is jerking off. Grunt, groan, grunt, on to the prison floor ... aaaagh! He seeds dragons' teeth. Out of each ejaculation spring up a swarm of fully-armed, mad-eyed homunculi. Everything is about to succumb to delirium.

Heedless of all this, Poe's future mother skipped on to a stage in the fresh-hatched American republic to sing an old-world ballad clad in the pretty rags of a ballet gypsy. Her dancer's grace, piping treble, dark curls, rosy cheeks – cute kid! And eyes with something innocent, something appealing in them that struck directly to the heart so that the smoky auditorium broke out in raucous sentimental cheers for her and clapped its leather palms together with a will. A star was born that night in the rude firmament of fit-ups and candle-footlights, but she was to be a shooting star; she flickered briefly in the void, she continued the inevitable trajectory of the meteor, downward. She hit the boards and trod them.

But, well after puberty, she was still able, thanks to her low stature and slim build, to continue to personate children, clever little ducks and prattlers of both sexes. Yet she was versatility personified; she could do you Ophelia, too.

She had a low, melodious voice of singular sweetness, an excellent thing in a woman. When crazed Ophelia handed round the rosemary and rue and sang: 'He is dead and gone, lady,' not a dry eye in the house, I assure you. She also tried her hand at Juliet and Cordelia and, if necessary, could personate the merriest soubrette; even when racked by the nauseas of her pregnancies, still she would smile, would smile and oh! the dazzling candour of her teeth!

Out popped her firstborn, Henry; her second, Edgar, came jostling after to share her knee with her scripts and suckle at her bosom while she learned her lines, yet she was always word-perfect even when she played two parts in the one night, Ophelia or Juliet and then, say, Little Pickle, the cute kid in the afterpiece, for the audiences of those days refused to leave the theatre after a tragedy unless the players changed costumes and came back to give them a little something extra to cheer them up again.

Little Pickle was a trousers' role. She ran back to the green-room and undid the top buttons of her waistcoat to let out a sore, milky breast to pacify little Edgar who, wakened by the hoots and catcalls that had greeted her too voluptuous imitation of a boy, likewise howled and screamed.

A mug of porter or a bottle of whisky stood on the dressing-table all the time. She dipped a plug of cotton in whisky and gave it to Edgar to suck when he would not stop crying.

The father of her children was a bad actor and only ever carried a spear in the many companies in which she worked. He often stayed behind in the green-room to look after the little ones. David Poe tipped a tumbler of neat gin to Edgar's lips to keep him quiet. The red-eyed Angel of Intemperance hopped out of the bottle of ardent spirits and snuggled down in little Edgar's longclothes. Meanwhile, on stage, her final child, in utero, stitched its flesh and bones together as best it could under the corset that preserved the theatrical illusion of Mrs Elizabeth Poe's eighteen inch waist until the eleventh hour, the tenth month.

Applause rocked round the wooden O. Loving mother that she was – for we have no reason to believe that she was not – Mrs Poe exited the painted scene to cram her jewels on her knee while tired tears ran rivers through her rouge and splashed upon their peaky faces. The monotonous clamour of their parents' argument sent them at last to sleep but the unborn one in the womb pressed its transparent hands over its vestigial ears in terror.

(To be born at all might be the worst thing.)

However, born at last this last child was, one July afternoon in a cheap theatrical boarding-house in New York City after many hours on a rented bed while flies buzzed at the windowpanes. Edgar and Henry, on a pallet on the floor, held hands. The midwife had to use a pair of blunt iron tongs to scoop out the reluctant wee thing; the sheet was tented up over Mrs Poe's lower half for modesty so the toddlers saw nothing except the midwife brandishing her dreadful instrument and then they heard the shrill cry of the new-born in the exhausted silence, like the sound of the blade of a skate on ice, and something bloody as a fresh-pulled tooth twitched between the midwife's pincers.

It was a girl.

David Poe spent his wife's confinement in a nearby tavern, wetting the baby's head. When he came back and saw the mess he vomited.

Then, before his sons' bewildered eyes, their father began to grow insubstantial. He unbecame. All at once he lost his outlines and began to waver on the air. It was twilit evening. Mama slept on the bed with a fresh mauve bud of flesh in a basket on the chair beside her. The air shuddered with the beginning of absence.

He said not one word to his boys but went on evaporating until he melted clean away, leaving behind him in the room as proof he had been there only a puddle of puke on the splintered floorboards.

As soon as the deserted wife got out of bed, she posted down to Virginia with her howling brats because she was booked for a tour of the South and she had no money put away so all the babies got to eat was her sweat. She dragged them with her in a trunk to Charleston; to Norfolk; then back to Richmond.

Down there, it is the foetid height of summer.

Stripped to her chemise in the airless dressing-room, she milks her sore breasts into a glass; this latest baby must be weaned before its mother dies.

She coughed. She slapped more, yet more rouge on her now haggard cheekbones. 'My children! what will become of my children?' Her eyes glittered and soon acquired a febrile brilliance that was not of *this* world. Soon she needed no rouge at all; red spots brighter than rouge appeared of their own accord on her cheeks while veins as blue as those in Stilton cheese but muscular, palpitating, prominent, lithe, stood out of her forehead. In Little Pickle's vest and breeches it was not now possible for her to create the least suspension of disbelief and something desperate, something fatal in her distracted playing both fascinated and appalled the witnesses, who could have thought they saw the living features of death itself upon her face. Her mirror, the actress' friend, the magic mirror in which she sees whom she has become, no longer acknowledged any but a death's head.

The moist, sullen, Southern winter signed her quietus. She put on Ophelia's madwoman's nightgown for her farewell.

When she summoned him, the spectral horseman came. Edgar looked out of the window and saw him. The soundless hooves of black-plumed horses struck sparks from the stones in the road outside. 'Father!' said Edgar; he thought their father must have reconstituted himself at this last extremity in order to transport them all to a better place but, when he looked more closely, by the light of a gibbous moon, he saw the sockets of the coachman's eyes were full of worms.

They told her children that now she could come back to take no curtain-calls no matter how fiercely all applauded the manner of her going. Lovers of the theatre plied her hearse with bouquets: 'And from her pure and uncorrupted flesh May violets spring.' (Not a dry eye in the house.) The three orphaned infants were dispersed into the bosoms of charitable protectors. Each gave the clay-cold cheek a final kiss; then they too kissed and parted, Edgar from Henry, Henry from the tiny one who did not move or cry but lay still and kept her eyes tight shut. When shall these three meet again? The church bell tolled: never never never never never.

Kind Mr Allan of Virginia, Edgar's own particular benefactor, who would buy his bread, henceforward, took his charge's little hand and led him from the funeral. Edgar parted his name in the middle to make room for Mr Allan inside it. Edgar was then three years old. Mr Allan ushered him into Southern affluence, down there; but do not think his mother left Edgar empty handed, although the dead actress was able to leave him only what could not be taken away from him, to wit, a few tattered memories.

TESTAMENT OF MRS ELIZABETH POE

Item: nourishment. A tit sucked in a green-room, the dug snatched away from the toothless lips as soon as her cue came, so that, of nourishment, he would retain only the memory of hunger and thirst endlessly unsatisfied.

Item: transformation. This is a more ambivalent relic. Something like this . . . Edgar would lie in prop-baskets on heaps of artificial finery and watch her while she painted her face. The candles made a profane altar of the mirror in which her vague face swam like a magic fish. If you caught hold of it, it would make your dreams come true but Mama slithered through all the nets which desire set out to catch her.

She stuck glass jewels in her ears, pinned back her nut-brown hair and tied a muslin bandage round her head, looking like a corpse for a minute. Then on went the yellow wig. Now you see her, now you don't; brunette turns blonde in the wink of an eye.

Mama turns round to show how she has changed into the lovely lady he glimpsed in the mirror.

'Don't touch me, you'll mess me.'

And vanishes in a susurration of taffeta.

Item: that women possess within them a cry, a thing that needs to be extracted . . . but this is only the dimmest of memories and will reassert itself in vague shapes of unmentionable dread only at the prospect of carnal connection.

Item: the awareness of mortality. For, as soon as her last child was born, if not before, she started to rehearse in private the long part of dying; once she began to cough she had no option.

Item: a face, the perfect face of a tragic actor, his face, white skin stretched tight over fine, white bones in a final state of wonderfully lucid emaciation.

Ignited by the tossed butt of a still-smouldering cigar that lodged in the cracks of the uneven floorboards, the theatre at Richmond where Mrs Poe had made her last appearance burned to the ground three weeks after her death. Ashes. Although Mr Allan told Edgar how all of his mother that was mortal had been buried in her coffin, Edgar knew the somebody elses she so frequently became lived in her dressing-table mirror and were not constrained by the physical laws that made her body rot. But now the mirror, too, was gone; and all the lovely and untouchable, volatile, unreal mothers went up together in a puff of smoke on a pyre of props and painted scenery.

The sparks from this conflagration rose high in the air, where they lodged in the sky to become a constellation of stars which only Edgar saw and then only on certain still nights of summer, those hot, rich, blue, mellow nights the slaves brought with them from Africa, weather that ferments the music of exile, weather of heartbreak and fever. (Oh, those voluptuous nights, like something forbidden!) High in the sky these invisible stars marked the points of a face folded in sorrow.

NATURE OF THE THEATRICAL ILLUSION: everything you see is false.

Consider the theatrical illusion with special reference to this impressionable child, who was exposed to it at an age when there is no reason for anything to be real.

He must often have toddled on to the stage when the theatre was empty and the curtains down so all was like a parlour prepared for a séance, waiting for the moment when the eyes of the observers make the mystery.

Here he will find a painted backdrop of, say, an antique castle – a castle! such as they don't build here; a Gothic castle all complete with owls and ivy. The flies are painted with segments of trees, massy oaks or something like that, all in two dimensions. Artificial shadows fall in all the wrong places. Nothing is what it seems. You knock against a gilded throne or horrid rack that looks perfectly solid, thick, immoveable, and you kick it sideways, it turns out to be made of papier mâché, it is as light as air – a child, you yourself, could pick it up and carry it off with you and sit in it and be a king or lie in it and be in pain.

A creaking, an ominous rattling scares the little wits out of you; when you jump round to see what is going on behind your back, why, the very castle is in mid-air! Heave-ho and up she rises, amid the inarticulate cries and muttered oaths of the stagehands, and down comes Juliet's tomb or Ophelia's sepulchre, and a super scuttles in, clutching Yorrick's skull.

The foul-mouthed whores who dandle you on their pillowy laps and tip mugs of sour porter against your lips now congregate in the wings, where they have turned into nuns or something. On the invisible side of the plush curtain that cuts you off from the beery, importunate, tobacco-stained multitude that has paid its pennies on the nail to watch these transcendent rituals now come the thumps, bangs and clatter that make the presence of their expectations felt. A stage-hand swoops down to scoop you up and carry you off, protesting, to where Henry, like a good boy, is already deep in his picture book and there is a poke of candy for you and the corner of a handkerchief dipped in moonshine and Mama in crown and train presses her rouged lips softly on your forehead before she goes down before the mob.

On his brow her rouged lips left the mark of Cain.

Having, at an impressionable age, seen with his own eyes the nature of the mystery of the castle – that all its horrors are so much painted cardboard and yet they terrify you – he saw another mystery and made less sense of it.

Now and then, as a great treat, if he kept quiet as a mouse, because he begged and pleaded so, he was allowed to stay in the wings and watch; the round-eyed baby saw that Ophelia could, if necessary, die twice nightly. All her burials were premature.

A couple of brawny supers carried Mama on stage in Act Four, wrapped in a shroud, tipped her into the cellarage amidst displays of grief from all concerned but up she would pop at curtain call having shaken the dust off her graveclothes and touched up her eye make-up, to curtsey with the rest of the resurrected immortals, all of whom, even Prince Hamlet himself, turned out, in the end, to be just as un-dead as she.

How could he, then, truly believe she would not come again, although, in the black suit that Mr Allan provided for him out of charity, he toddled behind her coffin to the cemetery? Surely, one fine day, the spectral coachman would return again, climb down from his box, throw open the carriage door and out she would step wearing the white nightdress in which he had last seen her, although he hoped this garment had been laundered in the interim since he last saw it all bloody from a haemorrhage.

Then a transparent constellation in the night sky would blink out; the scattered atoms would reassemble themselves to the entire and perfect Mama and he would run directly to her arms.

It is the mid-morning of the nineteenth century. He grows up under the black stars of the slave states. He flinches from that part of women the sheet hid. He becomes a man.

As soon as he becomes a man, affluence departs from Edgar. The heart and pocketbook that Mr Allan opened to the child now pull themselves together to expell. Edgar shakes the dust of the sweet South off his heels. He hies north, up here, to seek his fortune in the places where the light does not permit that chiaroscuro he loves; now Edgar Poe must live by his disordered wits.

The dug was snatched from the milky mouth and tucked away inside the bodice; the mirror no longer reflected Mama but, instead, a perfect stranger. He offered her his hand; smiling a tranced smile, she stepped out of the frame.

'My darling, my sister, my life and my bride!'

He was not put out by the tender years of this young girl whom he soon married; was she not just Juliet's age, just thirteen summers?

The magnificent tresses forming great shadowed eaves above her high forehead were the raven tint of nevermore, black as his suits the seams of which his devoted mother-in-law painted with ink so that they would not advertise to the world the signs of wear and, nowadays, he always wore a suit of sables, dressed in readiness for the next funeral in a black coat buttoned up to the stock and he never betrayed his absolute mourning by so much as one flash of white shirtfront. Sometimes, when his wife's mother was not there to wash and starch his linen, he economised on laundry bills and wore no shirt at all.

His long hair brushes the collar of this coat, from which poverty has worn off the nap. How sad his eyes are; there is too much of sorrow in his infrequent smile to make you happy when he smiles at you and so much of bitter gall, also, that you might mistake his smile for a grimace or a *grue* except when he smiles at his young wife with her forehead like a tombstone. Then he will smile and smile with as much posthumous tenderness as if he saw already: *Dearly beloved wife of* . . . carved above her eyebrows.

For her skin was white as marble and she was called – would you believe! – 'Virginia', a name that suited his expatriate's nostalgia and also her condition, for the childbride would remain a virgin until the day she died.

Imagine the sinless children lying in bed together! The pity of it!

For did she not come to him stiffly armoured in taboos – taboos against the violation of children; taboos against the violation of the dead – for, not to put too fine a point on it, didn't she always look like a walking corpse? But such a pretty, pretty corpse!

And, besides, isn't an undemanding, economic, decorative corpse the perfect wife for a gentleman in reduced circumstances, upon whom the four walls of paranoia are always about to converge?

Virginia Clemm. In the dialect of northern England, to be 'clemmed' is to be very cold. 'I'm fair clemmed.' Virginia Clemm.

She brought with her a hardy, durable, industrious mother of her own, to clean and cook and keep accounts for them and to outlive them, and to outlive them both.

Virginia was not very clever; she was by no means a sad case of arrested development, like his real, lost sister, whose life passed in a dream of non-being in her adopted home, the vegetable life of one who always declined to participate, a bud that never opened. (A doom lay upon them; the brother, Henry, soon died.) But the slow years passed and Virginia stayed as she had been at thirteen, a simple little thing whose sweet disposition was his only comfort and who never ceased to lisp, even when she started to rehearse the long part of dying.

She was light on her feet as a revenant. You would have thought she never bent a stem of grass as she passed across their little garden. When she spoke, when she sang, how sweet her voice was; she kept her harp in their cottage parlour, which her mother swept and polished until all was like a new pin. A few guests gathered there to partake of the Poes' modest hospitality. There was his brilliant conversation though his women saw to it that only tea was served, since all knew his dreadful weakness for liquor, but Virginia poured out with so much simple grace that everyone was charmed.

They begged her to take her seat at her harp and accompany herself in an Old World ballad or two. Eddy nodded gladly: 'yes', and she lightly struck the strings with white hands of which the long, thin fingers were so fine and waxen that you would have thought you could have set light to the tips to make of her hand the flaming Hand of Glory that casts all the inhabitants of the house, except the magician himself, into a profound and death-like sleep.

She sings: *Cold blows the wind, tonight, my love,*
        And a few drops of rain.

With a taper made from a manuscript folded into a flute, he slyly takes a light from the fire.

        I never had but one true love
        In cold earth she was lain.

He sets light to her fingers, one after the other.

        A twelve month and a day being gone
        The dead began to speak.

Eyes close. Her pupils contain in each a flame.

Who is that sitting on my grave
Who will not let me sleep?

All sleep. Her eyes go out. She sleeps.

He rearranges the macabre candelabra so that the light from her glorious hand will fall between her legs and then he busily turns back her petticoats; the mortal candles shine. Do not think it is not love that moves him; only love moves him.

He feels no fear.

An expression of low cunning crosses his face. Taking from his back pocket a pair of enormous pliers, he now, one by one, one by one by one, extracts the sharp teeth just as the midwife did.

All silent, all still.

Yet, even as he held aloft the last fierce canine in triumph above her prostrate and insensible form in the conviction he had at last exorcised the demons from desire, his face turned ashen and sear and he was overcome with the most desolating anguish to hear the rumbling of the wheels outside. Unbidden, the coachman came; the grisly emissary of her high-born kinsman shouted imperiously: 'Overture and beginners, please!' She popped the plug of spiritous linen between his lips; she swept off with a hiss of silk.

The sleepers woke and told him he was drunk; but his Virginia breathed no more!

After a breakfast of red-eye, as he was making his toilet before the mirror, he suddenly thought he would shave off his moustache in order to become a different man so that the ghosts who had persistently plagued him since his wife's death would no longer recognise him and would leave him alone. But, when he was clean-shaven, a black star rose in the mirror and he saw that his long hair and face folded in sorrow had taken on such a marked resemblance to that of his loved and lost one that he was struck like a stock or stone, with the cut-throat razor in his hand.

And, as he continued, fascinated, appalled, to stare in the reflective glass at those features that were his own and yet not his own, the bony casket of his skull began to agitate itself as if he had succumbed to a tremendous attack of the shakes.

Goodnight, sweet prince.

He was shaking like a backcloth about to be whisked off into oblivion.

Lights! he called out.

Now he wavered; horrors! *He was starting to dissolve*!

Lights! more lights! he cried, like the hero of a Jacobean tragedy when the murdering begins, for the black star was engulfing him.

On cue, the laser light on the Republic blasts him.

His dust blows away on the wind.

Overture and Incidental Music for
A Midsummer Night's Dream

———————

"Call me the Golden Herm.

My mother bore me in the Southern wild but, 'she, being mortal, of that boy did die,' as my Aunt Titania says, though 'boy' in the circumstances is pushing it, a bit, she's censoring me, there, she's rendering me unambiguous in order to get the casting director out of a tight spot. For 'boy' is correct, as far as it goes, but insufficient. Nor is the sweet South in the least wild, oh, dear, no! It is the lovely land where the lemon trees grow, multiplied far beyond the utmost reaches of your stultified Europocentric imaginations. Child of the sun am I, and of the breezes, juicy as mangoes, that mythopoeically caress the Coast of Coramandel far away on the porphyry and lapis lazuli Indian shore where everything is bright and precise as lacquer.

My Aunt Titania. Not, I should assure you, my *natural* aunt, no blood bond, no knot of the umbilical in the connection, but my mother's best friend, to whom, before she departed, she entrusted me, and, therefore, always called by me 'auntie'.

Titania, she, the great fat, showy, pink and blonde thing, the Memsahib, I call her, Auntie Tit-tit-tit-ania (for her tits are the things you notice first, size of barrage balloons), Tit-tit-tit-omania boxed me up in a trunk she bought from the Army and Navy Stores, labelled it 'Wanted on Voyage' (oh, yes, indeed!) and shipped me here.

Here! to – ATISHOO! – catch my death of cold in this dripping bastard wood. Rain, rain, rain, rain, rain!

'Flaming June', the sarcastic fairies mutter, looking glum, as well they might, poor dears, their little wings all sodden and plastered to their backs, so water-logged they can hardly take off and no sooner airborne than they founder in the pelting downpour, crash-land among the plashy bracken furls amid much piteous squeaking. 'Never such weather,' complain the fairies, amid the brakes of roses putting on – I must admit – a brave if pastel-coloured floral show amidst the inclemency of the weather, and the flat dishes of the pale wild roses spill over with the raindrops that have collected upon them as the bushes shudder in the reverberations of dozens and dozens of teeny tiny sneezes, for no place on their weeny anatomies to store a handkerchief and all the fairies have got shocking colds as well as I.

Nothing in my princely, exquisite, peacock-jewelled heredity prepared me for the dank, grey, English midsummer. A midsummer nightmare, I call it. The whirling winds have wrenched the limbs off even the hugest oaks and brought down altogether the more tottery elms so that they sprawl like collapsed drunks athwart dishevelled fairy rings. Thunder, lightning, and, at night, the blazing stars whizz down and bomb the wood ... nothing temperate about your temperate climate, dear, I snap at Aunt Titania, but she blames it all on Uncle Oberon, whose huff expresses itself in thunder and he makes it rain when he abuses himself, which it would seem he must do almost all the time, thinking of me, the while, no doubt. Of ME!

> For Oberon is passing fell and wrath
> Because that she, as her attendant hath
> A lovely boy, stolen from an Indian king;
> She never had so sweet a changeling;
> And jealous Oberon would have the child!

'Boy' again, see; which isn't the half of it. Misinformation. The patriarchal version. No king had nothing to do with it; it was all between my mother and my auntie, wasn't it.

Besides, is a child to be stolen? Or given? Or taken? Or sold in bondage, dammit? Are these blonde English fairies the agents of proto-colonialism?

To all this, in order to preserve my complicated integrity, I present a façade of passive opposition. I am here. I am.

I am Herm, short for *hermaphrodite verus*, one testis, one ovary, half of each but all complete and more, much more, than the sum of my parts. This elegantly retractable appendage, here ... is *not* the tribade's well-developed clit, but the veritable reproductive erectile tissue, while the velvet-lipped and deliciously closable aperture below it is, I assure you, a viable avenue of the other gender. So there.

Take a look. I'm not shy. Impressive, huh?

And I am called, the Golden Herm, for I am gold all over; when I was born, wee, tiny, playful cherubs filled their cheeks and lungs and blew, blew the papery sheets of beaten gold all over my infant limbs, to which they stuck and clung. See me shine!

And here I stand, under the dripping trees, in the long, rank, soaking grass among draggletail dog-daisies and the branched candelabras of the buttercups from whom the gusty rain has knocked off all the petals, leaving their warty green heads bald. And the bloody crane's bill. And the stinging nettles, those Portuguese men-o'-war of the woodland, who gave me so many nasty shocks when I first met them. And pease-blossom and mustard-seed and innumerable unknown-to-me weeds, the dreary, washed-out, pinks, yellows and Cambridge blues of them. Boring. In the underpinnings of the trees, all soggy and floral as William Morris newspaper in an abandoned house, I, in order to retain my equilibrium and psychic balance, meditate in the yogic posture known as The Tree, that is, on one leg.

Bearer of both arrow and target, wound and bow, spoon and porringer, in my left hand I hold a lotus, looking a bit the worse for wear by now. My snake coils round my other arm.

I am golden, stark naked and bi-partite.

On my golden face, a fixed, archaic grin. Except when –

ATISHOO!

Damn' occidental common cold virus.

ATISHOO."

The Golden Herm stood in the green wood.

This wood is, of course, nowhere near Athens; the script is a positive maze of false leads. The wood is really located somewhere in the English midlands, possibly near Bletchley, where the great decoding machine was sited. Correction: this wood *was* located in the English midlands until oak, ash and thorn were chopped down to make room for a motorway a few years ago. However, since the wood existed only as a structure of the imagination, in the first place, it will remain, in the second place, as a green, decorative margin to the eternity the poet promised for himself. The English poet; his is, essentially, an English wood. It is *the* English wood.

The English wood is nothing like the dark, necromantic forest in which the Northern European imagination begins and ends, where its dead and the witches live, and Baba-yaga stalks about in her house with chicken's feet looking for children in order to eat them. No. There is a qualitative, not a quantitive, difference between this wood and that forest. The difference does not exist just because a wood contains fewer trees than a forest and covers less ground. That is just one of the causes of the difference and does not explain the effects of the difference.

For example, an English wood, however marvellous, however metamorphic, cannot, by definition, be trackless, although it might well be formidably labyrinthine. Yet there is always a way out of a maze, and, even if you cannot find it for a while, you know that it is there. A maze is a construct of the human mind, and not unlike it; lost in the wood, this analogy will always console. But to be lost in the forest is to be lost to *this* world, to be abandoned by the light, to lose yourself utterly with no guarantee you will either find yourself or else be found, to be committed against your will – or, worse, of your own desire – to a perpetual absence from humanity, an existential catastrophe, for the forest is as infinitely boundless as the human heart.

But the wood is finite, a closure; you purposely mislay your way in the wood, for the sake of the pleasure of roving, the temporary confusion of direction is in the nature of a holiday from which you will come home refreshed, with your pockets full of nuts, your hands full of wildflowers and the cast feather of a bird in your cap. That forest is haunted; this wood is enchanted.

The very perils of the wood, so many audio-visual aids to a pleasurable titillation of mild fear; the swift rattle of an ascending pheasant, velvet thud of an owl, red glide of the fox – these may all 'give you a fright', but, here, neither hobgoblin nor foul fiend can daunt your spirit because the English lobs and hobs reflect nothing more than a secular faith in the absence of harm in nature, part of the credit sheet of a temperate climate. (Hear that, Herm? No tigers burn bright, here; no scaly pythons, no armoured scorpions.) Since the last English wolf was killed, there is nothing savage among the trees to terrify you. All is mellow in the filtered light, where Robin Wood, the fertility spirit, lurks in the green shade; this wood is kind to lovers.

Indeed, you might call the wood the common garden of the village, a garden almost as intentionally wild as one of Bacon's 'natural wildernesses', where every toad carries a jewel in its head and all the flowers have names, nothing is unknown – this kind of wilderness is not an otherness.

And always something to eat! Mother Nature's greengrocery store; sorrel for soup, mushrooms, dandelion and chickweed – there's your salad, mint and thyme for seasoning, wild strawberries and black-berries and, in the autumn, a plenitude of nuts. Nebuchadnezzar, in an English wood, need not have confined his appetite to grass.

The English wood offers us a glimpse of a green, unfallen world a little closer to Paradise than we are.

Such is the English wood in which we see the familiar fairies, the blundering fiancés, the rude mechanicals. This is the true Shakespearian wood – but it is not the wood of Shakespeare's time, which did not know itself to be Shakespearian, and therefore felt no need to keep up appearances. No. The wood we have just described is that of nineteenth-century nostalgia, which disinfected the wood, cleansing it of the grave, hideous and elemental beings with which the superstition of an earlier age had filled it. Or, rather, denaturing, castrating these beings until they came to look just as they do in those photographs of fairy folk that so enraptured Conan Doyle. It is Mendelssohn's wood.

'Enter these enchanted woods . . . ' who could resist such a magical invitation?

However, as it turns out, the Victorians did not leave the woods in quite the state they might have wished to find them.

The Puck was obsessively fascinated by the exotic visitor. In some respects, it was the attraction of opposites, for, whereas the Golden Herm was sm-o-o-o-th, the Puck was hairy. On these chill nights of June, Puck inside his hairy pelt was the only one kept warm at all. Hairy. Shaggy. Especially about the thighs. (And, h'm, on the palms of his hands.)

Shaggy as a Shetland pony when naked and sometimes goes on all fours. When he goes on all fours, he whinnies; or else he barks.

He is the lub, the lubber fiend, and sometimes he plays at being the nut-brown house-sprite for whom a bowl of milk is left outside the door, although, if you want to be rid of him, you must leave him a pair of trousers; he thinks a gift of trousers is an insult to his sex, of which he is most proud. Nesting in his luxuriant pubic curls, that gleam with the deep-fried gloss of the woodcarvings of Grinling Gibbons, see his testicles, wrinkled ripe as medlars.

Puck loves hokey-pokey and peek-a-boo. He has relations all over the place – in Iceland, the *puki*; the Devonshire *pixy*; the *spook* of the Low Countries are all his next of kin and not one of them is up to any good. That Puck!

The tender little exiguities that cluster round the Queen of the Fairies do not like to play with the Puck because he is so rough and rips their painted wings in games of tag and pulls the phantasmal legs off the grey gnats that draw Titania's wee coach through the air, kisses the girls and makes them cry, creeps up and swings between the puce, ithyphallic foxglove spires above Titania's bed so the raindrops fall and scatter in a drenching shower and up she wakes. Spiteful!

Puck is no more polymorphously perverse than all the rest of these sub-microscopic particles, his peers, yet there is something particularly rancid and offensive about his buggery and his undinism and his frotteurism and his scopophilia and his – indeed, my very paper would *blush*, go pink as an invoice, should I write down upon it some of the things Puck gets up to down in the reeds by the river, as he is distantly related to the great bad god Pan and, when in the mood, behaves in a manner uncommon in an English wood, although familiar in the English public school.

By the Puck's phallic orientation, you know him for a creature of King Oberon's.

Hairy Puck fell in love with Golden Herm and often came to frolic round the lovely living statue in the moonlit glade, although he could not, happily for the Herm, get near enough to touch because Titania forethoughtfully had thrown a magical *cordon sanitaire* around her lovely adoptive, so that s/he was, as it were, in an invisible glass case, such as s/he might find herself, some centuries later, in the Victoria and Albert Museum. Against this transparent, intangible barrier, the Puck often flattened still further his already snub nose.

The Herm removed his/her left foot from its snug nest in her/his crotch and placed it on the ground. With one single, fluent, gracile movement of transition, s/he shifted on to the *other* leg. The lotus and the snake, on either arm, stayed where they were.

The Puck, pressed tight against Titania's magic, sighed heavily, stepped back a few paces and began energetically to play with himself.

Have *you* seen fairy sperm? We mortals call it, cuckoo spit.

And no passing, clayey mortal, tramping through the wood on great, heavy feet, scattering the fairies who twitter like bats in their fright, just as such a mortal could never hear them, so he would never spot the unafraid Herm, sticking stock still as a trance.

And if you *did* chance to spy him/her, you would think the little yellow idol was a talisman dropped from a gypsy pocket, perhaps, or a charm fallen off a girl's bracelet, or else the gift from inside a very expensive cracker.

Yet, if you picked up the beautiful object and held it on the palm of your hand, you would feel how warm it was, as if somebody had been holding it tight before you came and only just put it down.

And, if you watched long enough, you would see the golden sequins of the eyelids move.

At which a wind of strangeness would rise and blow away the wood and all within it.

Just as your shadow can grow big and then shrink to almost nothing, and then swell up, again, so can *these* shadows, these insubstantial bubbles of the earth, these 'beings' to whom the verb, 'to be', may not be properly applied, since, in our sense, they are not. They *cannot* be; they cannot cast their own shadows, for who has seen the shadow of a shadow? Their existences are necessarily moot – do *you* believe in fairies? Their lives lead always just teasingly almost out of the corners of the eyes of their observers, so it is possible they were only, all the time, a trick of the light . . . such half-being, with such a lack of public acknowledgement, is not conducive to any kind of visual consistency among them. So they may take what shapes they please.

The Puck can turn himself into anything he likes: a three-legged stool, in order to perpetrate the celebrated trick ('Then slip I from her bum, down topples she') so beloved in the lower forms of grammar schools when the play is read aloud round the class because it is suitable for children because it is about fairies; a baby Fiat; a grand piano; anything!

Except the lover of the Golden Herm.

In his spare moments, when he was not off about his Master's various businesses, the Puck, wistfully lingering outside the Herm's magic circle like an urchin outside a candy shop, concluded that, in order to take full advantage of the sexual facilities offered him by the Herm, should the barrier between them ever be removed – and, unlikely as this eventuality might be, the Puck's motto was 'Be Prepared'! – if there was to be intercourse between himself and the Golden Herm, then the Herm's partner would require a similar set of equipment to the Herm in order to effect maximally satisfactory congress.

Then the Puck further concluded that the equipment of the Herm's hypothetical partner would need, however, to be attached in *reversed order* to that of the Herm, in order to procure a perfect fit and no fumbling; the Puck, a constant inquisitive spy on mortal couples come to make the beast with two backs in what they mistakenly believed to be privacy, had noticed there is a vexed question of handedness about caresses, so that all right-handed lovers truly require left-handed lovers during the preliminaries to the act, and Mother Nature, when she cast the human mould, took no account of foreplay, which alone distinguishes us from the beasts when we are being beastly.

Try, try as he might, try and try again, the Puck could not get it quite right, although, after strenuous effort, he at last succeeded in turning himself into a perfect simulacrum of the Herm and would, at odd moments, adopt the Herm's form and posture and stand facing him in the wood, a living mirror of the living statue, except for the fierce erection the satyromaniac Puck could not subdue when in the presence of his love.

The Herm continued to smile inscrutably, except when he sneezed.

But all of them can grow BIG! then shrink down to . . . the size of dots, of less than dots, again. Every last one of them is of such elastic – since incorporeal – substance. Consider the Queen of the Fairies.

Her very name, Titania, bears witness to her descent from the giant race of the Titans; and 'descend' might seem apt enough, at first, to describe the declension when she manifests herself under her alias, Mab, or, in Wales, Mabh, and rules over the other diminutives, herself the size of the solitaire in an engagement ring, as infinitely little as her forebears were infinitely large.

'Now, I do call my horned master, the Horn of Plenty, but as for my missus –' said the Puck, in his inimitable Worcestershire drawl.

Like a Japanese water-flower dropped in a glass of water, Titania grows . . .

In the dewy wood tinselled with bewildering moonlight, the bumbling, tumbling babies of the fairy crèche trip over the hem of her dress, which is no more nor less than the margin of the wood itself; they stumble in the tangled grass as they play with the coneys, the quick brown fox-cubs, the russet field mice and the wee scraps of grey voles, blind velvet Mole and striped Brock with his questing snout – all the denizens of the woodland are her embroiderings, and the birds flutter round her head, settle on her shoulders and make their nests in her great abundance of disordered hair, in which are plaited poppies and the ears of wheat.

The arrival of the Queen is announced by no fanfare of trumpets but the ash-soft lullaby of wood doves and the liquid coloratura blackbird. Moonlight falls like milk upon her naked breasts.

She is like a double bed; or, a table laid for a wedding breakfast; or, a fertility clinic.

In her eyes are babies. When she looks at you, you helplessly reduplicate. Her eyes provoke engendering.

Correction: used to provoke.

But not *this* year. Frosts have blasted the fruit blossom, rain has rotted all the corn so her garland is not gold but greenish and phosphorescent with blight. The acres of the rye have been invaded with ergot and, this year, eating bread will make you mad. The floods broke down the Bridge of Ware. The beasts refuse to couple; the cow rejects the bull and the bull keeps himself to himself. Even the goats, hitherto synonymous with lechery, prefer to curl up with a good book. The very worms no longer agitate the humus with their undulating and complex embraces. In the wood, a chaste, conventual calm reigns over everything, as if the foul weather had put everybody off.

The wonderful giantess manifested herself with an owl on her shoulder and an apron-full of roses and of babies so rosy the children could scarcely be distinguished from the flowers. She picked up her defunct friend's child, the Herm. The Herm stood on one leg on the palm of Titania's hand and smiled the inscrutable, if manic, smile of the figures in Hindu erotic sculpture.

'My husband shall not have you!' cried Titania. 'He shan't! *I* shall keep you!'

At that, thunder crashed, the heavens, which, for a brief moment, had sealed themselves up, now reopened again with redoubled fury, and all the drenched babies in Titania's pinafore coughed and sneezed. The worms in the rosebuds woke up at the clamour and began to gnaw.

But the Queen stowed the tiny Herm safe away between her breasts as if s/he were a locket and herself diminished until she was a suitable size to enjoy her niece or nephew or nephew/niece *à choix* in the obscurity of an acorn-cup.

'But she cannot put horns on her husband, for he is antlered, already,' opined the Puck, changing back into himself and skipping across the glade to the heels of his master. For no roe-buck now raises his head behind that gorse bush to watch these goings on; Oberon is antlered like a ten-point stag.

Among the props of the Globe Theatre, along with the thunder-making machine and the bearskins, is listed a 'robe for to go invisible'. By his coat, you understand that Oberon is to remain unseen as he broods magisterial but impotent above the scarcely discernable quiverings among last year's oak leaves that conceal his wife and the golden bone of contention that has come between the elemental lovers.

High in the thick of a dripping hedge of honeysuckle, a wee creature was extracting a tritonic, numinous, luxuriantly perfumed melody from the pan-pipes of the wild woodbine. The tune broke off as the player convulsed with ugly coughing. He gobbed phlegm, that flew through the air until its trajectory was interrupted by a cowslip, to whose freckled ear the translucent pustule clung. The infinitesimal then took up his tootling again.

The Herm's golden skin is made of beaten gold but the flesh beneath it has been marinated in: black pepper, red chilli, yellow turmeric, cloves, coriander, cumin, fenugreek, ginger, mace, nutmeg, allspice, khus-khus, garlic, tamarind, coconut, candlenut, lemon grass, galangel and now and then you get – phew! – a whiff of asafoetida. Hot stuff! Were the Herm to be served piled up on a lordly platter and garnished with shreds of its own outer casing, s/he would then resemble that royal dish, *moglai biriani*, which is decorated with edible gold shavings in order, so they say, to aid digestion. Nothing so deliciously aromatic as the Herm has ever been scented before in England's green and pleasant land, still labouring as it is at this point in time under its unrelieved late medieval diet of boiled cabbage. The Herm is hot and sweet as if drenched in sun and honey, but Oberon is the colour of ashes.

The Puck, tormented for lack of the Herm, pulled up a mandrake and sunk his prodigious tool in the cleft of the reluctant root, which shrieked mournfully but to no avail as old shaggylugs had his way with it.

Distemperate weather! It's raining, it's pouring; the earth is in estrangement from itself, the withered buds tumble out of the Queen's apron and rot on the mulch, for Oberon has put a stop to reproduction.

But still Titania hugs the Herm to her shrivelling bosoms and will not let her husband have the wee thing, not even for one minute. Did she not give a sacred promise to a friend?

What does the Herm want?

The Herm wants to know what 'want' means.

'I am unfamiliar with the concept of desire. I am the unique and perfect, paradigmatic Hermaphrodite, provoking on all sides desire yet myself transcendent, the unmoved mover, the still eye of the tempest, exemplary and self-sufficient, the beginning and the end.'

Titania, despairing of the Herm's male aspect, inserted a tentative forefinger in the female orifice. The Herm felt bored.

Oberon watched the oak leaves shiver and said nothing, for he was choked with balked longing for the golden, half and halfy thing with its salivatory perfume. He took off his invisible disguise and made himself gigantic and bulked up in the night sky over the wood, arms akimbo, blotting out the moon, naked but for his buskins and his great codpiece. The mossy antlers on his forehead aren't the half of it, he wears a crown made out of yellowish vertebrae of unmentionable mammals, down from beneath which his black hair drops straight as light. Since he is in his malign aspect, he has put on, furthermore, a necklace of suggestively little skulls, which might be those of the babies he has plucked from human cradles – do not forget, in German, they call him Erl-king.

His face, breast and thighs he has daubed with charcoal; Oberon, lord of night and silence, of the grave silence of endless night, Lord of Plutonic dark. His hair, long, it never saw scissors; but he has this peculiarity – no hair at all on either chop or chin, nor his shins, neither, but all his face bald as an egg except for the eyebrows, that meet in the middle.

Indeed, who in their right minds would trust a child to this man?

When Oberon cheers up a bit, he lets the sun come out and then he'll hang little silver bells along his codpiece and they go jingle jangle jingle when he walks up and down and round about, the pretty chinking sounds suspended wriggling in the air like homunculi wherever he has passed.

And if he is not a creature of the dream, then surely you have forgotten your dreams.

The Puck, too, yearning and thwarted as he was, found himself helplessly turning himself into the thing he longed for, and, under the faintly twitching oak leaves, became yellow, metallic, double-sexed and extravagantly precious-looking. There the Puck stood on one leg, the living image of the Herm, and glittered.

Oberon saw him.

Oberon stooped down and picked up the Puck and stood him, a simulated Yogic tree, on his palm. A misty look came into Oberon's eyes. The Puck knew he had no option but to go through with it.

ATISHOO!

Titania tenderly wiped the Herm's nose with the edge of her petticoat, on which the flowers are all drooping, shedding embroidery stitches, the fruits are cankering and spotting and coming undone for, if Oberon is the Horn of Plenty, then Titania is the Cauldron of Generation and, unless he gives her a stir, now and then, with his great pot stick, the cauldron will go off the boil.

Lie close and sleep, said Titania to the Herm. My fays shall lullaby you as we cuddle up on my mattress of dandelion down.

The draggled fairies obediently started in on a chorus of: 'Ye spotted snakes with double tongue,' but were all so afflicted by coughing and sneezing and rawness of the throat and rheumy eyes and gasping for breath and all the other symptoms of rampant influenza that their hoarse voices petered out before they reached the bit about the newts and after that the only sound in the entire wood was the pit-pattering of the rain on the leaves.

The orchestra has laid down its instruments. The curtain rises. The play begins.

The Kitchen Child

'Born in a trunk', they say when a theatrical sups grease-paint with mother's milk, and if there be a culinary equivalent of the phrase then surely I merit it, for was I not conceived the while a soufflé rose? A lobster soufflé, very choice, twenty-five minutes in a medium oven.

And the very first soufflé that ever in her life as cook me mam was called upon to make, ordered up by some French duc, house guest of Sir and Madam, me mam pleased as punch to fix it for him since few if any *fins becs* pecked their way to our house, not even during the two weeks of the Great Grouse Shoot when nobs rolled up in droves to score the feathered booty of the skies. Especially not then. Palates like shoe leather. 'Pearls before swine,' my mother would have said as she reluctantly sent the four and twenty courses of her Art up to the dining-room, except that pigs would have exhibited more gourmandise. I tell you, the English country house, yes! that's the place for grub; but, only when Sir and Madam are *pas chez lui*. It is the staff who keep up the standards.

For Madam would touch nothing but oysters and grapes on ice three times a day, due to the refinement of her sensibility, while Sir fasted until a devilled bone at sundown, his tongue having been burned out by curry when he was governing a bit of Poonah. (I reckon those Indians hotted up his fodder out of spite. Oh, the cook's vengeance, when it strikes – terrible!) And as for the Shooters of Grouse, all they wanted was sandwiches for hors d'oeuvres, sandwiches for entrées, followed by sandwiches, sandwiches, sandwiches, and their hip flasks kept replenished, oh, yes, wash it down with the amber fluid and who can tell how it tastes?

So me mam took great pains with the construction of this, her very first lobster soufflé, sending the boy who ground knives off on his bike to the sea, miles, for the beast itself and then the boiling of it alive, how it come squeaking piteously crawling out of the pot etc. etc. etc. so me mam all a-flutter before she so much as separated the eggs.

Then, just as she bent over the range to stir the flour into the butter, a pair of hands clasped tight around her waist. Thinking, at first, it was but kitchen horseplay, she twitched her ample hips to put him off as she slid the egg yolks into the roux. But as she mixed in the lobster meat, diced up, all nice, she felt those hands stray higher.

That was when too much cayenne went in. She always regretted that.

And as she was folding in the toppling contents of the bowl of beaten egg-white, God knows what it was he got up to but so much so she flings all into the white dish with abandon and:

'To hell with it!'

Into the oven goes the soufflé; the oven door slams shut.

I draw a veil.

'But, mam!' I often begged her. '*Who was that man?*'

'Lawks a mercy, child,' says she. 'I never thought to ask. I were that worried the wallop I give the oven door would bring the soufflé down.'

But, no. The soufflé went up like a montgolfier and, as soon as its golden head knocked imperiously against the oven door, she bust through the veil I have discreetly drawn over this scene of passion and emerged, smoothing her apron, in order to extract the exemplary dish amidst oohs and aahs of the assembled kitchen staff, some forty-five in number.

But not quite exemplary. The cook met her match in the eater. The housekeeper brings his plate herself, slaps it down. 'He said: "Trop de cayenne," and scraped it off his plate into the fire,' she announces with a gratified smirk. She is a model of refinement and always very particular about her aspirates. She hiccups. She even says the 'h' in 'hic'.

My mother weeps for shame.

'What we need here is a congtinental – hic – chef to improve *le ton*,' menaces the housekeeper, tossing me mam a killing look as she sweeps out the door for me mam is a simple Yorkshire lass for all she has magic in her fingers but no room for two queens in this hive, the housekeeper hates her. And the housekeeper is pricked perpetually by the fancy for the importation of a Carême or a Soyer with moustaches like hatracks to *croquembouche* her and *milly filly* her as is all the rage.

'For isn't it Alberlin, chef to the dear Devonshires; and Crépin, at the Duchess of Sutherland's. Then there's Labalme, with the Duke of Beaufort's household, doncherno . . . and the Queen, bless her, has her Ménager . . . while we're stuck with that fat cow who can't speak nothing but broad Yorkshire, never out of her carpet slippers . . .'

Conceived upon a kitchen table, born upon a kitchen floor; no bells rang to welcome me but, far more aptly, my arrival heralded by a bang! bang! bang! on every skillet in the place, a veritable fusillade of copper-bottom kitchen tympani; and the merry clatter of ladle against dish-cover; and the very turnspit dogs all went: 'Bow wow!'

It being, as you might yourself compute, a good three months off October, Sir and Madam being in London the housekeeper maintains a fine style all by herself, sitting in her parlour partaking of the best Bohea from a Meissen cup, to which she adds a judicious touch of rum from the locked bottles to which she's forged a key in her ample leisure. The housekeeper's little skivvy, that she keeps to fetch, carry and lick boot, just topping the teacup up with old Jamaica, all hell breaks loose below stairs as if a Chinese orchestra started up its woodblocks and xylophones, crash, wallop.

'What on earth are the – hic – lower ordures up to?' elocutes the housekeeper in ladylike and dulcet tones, giving the ear of the skivvy a quick but vicious tug to jerk the gossip out of her.

'Oh, madamissima!' quavers the poor little skivvyette. ''Tis nobbut the cook's babby!'

'The cook's baby?!?'

Due to my mother's corpulence, which is immense, she's round as the 'o' in 'obese', and the great loyalty and affection towards her of all the kitchen staff, the housekeeper knew nothing of my imminence but, amid her waxing wroth, also glad to hear it, since she thought she spied a way to relieve my mother of her post due to this unsolicited arrival and then nag Sir and Madam to get in some mincing and pomaded gent to *chaudfroid* and *gêlée* and butter up. Below stairs she descends forthwith, a stately yet none too stable progress due to the rum with a dash of tea she sips all day, the skivvy running in front of her to throw wide the door.

What a spectacle greets her! Raphael might have sketched it, had he been in Yorkshire at the time. My mother, wreathed in smiles, enthroned on a sack of spuds with, at her breast, her babe, all neatly swaddled in a new-boiled pudding cloth and the entire kitchen brigade arranged around her in attitudes of adoration, each brandishing a utensil and giving out therewith that merry rattle of the ladles, yours truly's first lullaby.

Alas, my cradle song soon peters out in the odd thwack and tinkle as the housekeeper casts her coldest eye.

'What's – hic – this?'

'A bonny boy!' croons me mam, planting a smacking kiss on the tender forehead pressed against her pillowing bosom.

'Out of the house for this!' cries the housekeeper. 'Hic,' she adds.

But what a clang and clamour she unleashes with that demand; as if she'd let off a bomb in a hardware store, for all present (except my mother and myself) attack their improvised instruments with renewed vigour, chanting in unison:

'The kitchen child! The kitchen child! You can't turn out the kitchen child!'

And that was the truth of the matter; who else could I claim as my progenitor if not the greedy place itself, that, if it did not make me, all the same, it caused me to be made? Not one scullery maid nor the littlest vegetable boy could remember who or what it was which visited my mother that soufflé morning, every hand in the kitchen called to cut sandwiches, but some fat shape seemed to have haunted the place, drawn to the kitchen as a ghost to the dark; had not that gourmet duc kept a gourmet valet? Yet his outlines melt like aspic in the heat from the range.

'The kitchen child!'

The kitchen brigade made such a din that the housekeeper retreated to revive herself with another tot of rum in her private parlour, for, faced with a mutiny amongst the pans, she discovered little valour in her spirit and went to sulk in her tent.

The first toys I played with were colanders, egg whisks and saucepan lids. I took my baths in the big tureen in which the turtle soup was served. They gave up salmon until I could toddle because, as for my crib, what else but the copper salmon kettle? And this kettle was stowed way up high on the mantelshelf so I could snooze there snug and warm out of harm's way, soothed by the delicious odours and appetising sounds of the preparation of nourishment, and there I cooed my way through babyhood above that kitchen as if I were its household deity high in my tiny shrine.

And, indeed, is there not something holy about a great kitchen? Those vaults of soot-darkened stone far above me, where the hams and strings of onions and bunches of dried herbs dangle, looking somewhat like the regimental banners that unfurl above the aisles of old churches. The cool, echoing flags scrubbed spotless twice a day by votive persons on their knees. The scoured gleam of row upon row of metal vessels dangling from hooks or reposing on their shelves till needed with the air of so many chalices waiting for the celebration of the sacrament of food. And the range like an altar, yes, an altar, before which my mother bowed in perpetual homage, a fringe of sweat upon her upper lip and fire glowing in her cheeks.

At three years old she gave me flour and lard and straightaway I invented shortcrust. I being too little to manage the pin, she hoists me on her shoulders to watch her as she rolls out the dough upon the marble slab, then sets me to stamp out the tartlets for myself, tears of joy at my precocity trickling down her cheeks, lets me dollop on the damson jam and lick the spoon for my reward. By three and a half, I've progressed to rough puff and, after that, no holding me. She perches me on a tall stool so I can reach to stir the sauce, wraps me in her pinny that goes round and round and round me thrice, tucks it in at the waist else I trip over it head first into my own Hollandaise. So I become her acolyte.

Reading and writing come to me easy. I learn my letters as follows: A for asparagus, *asperges au beurre fondue* (though never, for my mother's sake, with a *sauce bâtarde*); B for *boeuf*, baron of, roasted mostly, with a *pouding Yorkshire* patriotically sputtering away beneath it in the dripping pan; C for carrots, *carrottes*, *chouxfleur*, *camembert* and so on, right down to Zabaglione, although I often wonder what use the X might be, since it figures in no cook's alphabet.

And I stick as close to that kitchen as the croûte to a pâté or the mayonnaise to an oeuf. First, I stand on that stool to my saucepans; then on an upturned bucket; then on my own two feet. Time passes.

Life in this remote mansion flows by a tranquil stream, only convulsing into turbulence once a year and then for two weeks only, but that fuss enough, the Grouse Shoot, when they all come from town to set us by the ears.

Although Sir and Madam believe their visit to be the very and unique reason for the existences of each and every one of us, the yearly climacteric of our beings, when their staff, who, as far as *they* are concerned, sleep out a hibernation the rest of the year, now spring to life like Sleeping Beauty when her prince turns up, in truth, we get on so well without them during the other eleven and a half months that the arrival of Themselves is a chronic interruption of our routine. We sweat out the fortnight of their presence with as ill a grace as gentlefolk forced by reduced circumstances to take paying guests into their home, and as for haute cuisine, forget it; sandwiches, sandwiches, sandwiches, all they want is sandwiches.

And never again, ever again, a special request for a soufflé, lobster or otherwise. Me mam always a touch broody come the Grouse Shoot, moody, distracted, and, even though no order came, nevertheless, every year, she would prepare her lobster soufflé all the same, send the grinding boy off for the lobster, boil it alive, beat the eggs, make the panada etc. etc. etc., as if the doing of the thing were a magic ritual that would raise up out of the past the great question mark from whose loins her son had sprung so that, perhaps, she could get a good look at his face, this time. Or, perhaps, there was some other reason. But she never said either way. In due course, she could construct the airiest, most savoury soufflé that ever lobster graced; but nobody arrived to eat it and none of the kitchen had the heart. So, fifteen times in all, the chickens got that soufflé.

Until, one fine October day, the mist rising over the moors like the steam off a consommé, the grouse taking last hearty meals like condemned men, my mother's vigil was at last rewarded. The house party arrives and as it does we hear the faint, nostalgic wail of an accordion as a closed barouche comes bounding up the drive all festooned with the *lys de France*.

Hearing the news, my mother shakes, comes over queer, has to have a sit down on the marble pastry slab whilst I, oh, I prepare to meet my maker, having arrived at the age when a boy most broods about his father.

But what's this? Who trots into the kitchen to pick up the chest of ice the duc ordered for the bottles he brought with him but a beardless boy of my own age or less! And though my mother tries to quizz him on the whereabouts of some other hypothetical valet who, once upon a time, might possibly have made her hand tremble so she lost control of the cayenne, he claims he cannot understand her Yorkshire brogue, he shakes his head, he mimes incomprehension. Then, for the third time in all her life, my mother wept.

First, she wept for shame because she'd spoiled a dish. Next, she wept for joy, to see her son mould the dough. And now she weeps for absence.

But still she sends the grinding boy off for a lobster, for she must and will prepare her autumn ritual, if only as a wake for hope or as the funeral baked meats. And, taking matters into my own hands, I use the quickest method, the dumb waiter, above stairs to make a personal enquiry of this duc as to where his staff might be.

The duc, relaxing before dinner, popping a cork or two, is wrapped up in a velvet quilted smoking jacket much like the coats they put on very well-bred dogs, warming his slippered (Morocco) feet before the blazing fire and singing songs to himself in his native language. And I never saw a fatter man; he'd have given my mother a stone or two and not felt the loss. Round as the 'o' in 'rotund'. If he's taken aback by the apparition of this young chef out of the panelling, he's too much of a gent to show it by a jump or start, asks, what can he do for me? nice as you like and, in my best culinary French, my *petit poi de française*, I stammer out:

'The valet de chambre who accompanied you (garni de) those many years past of your last visit –'

'Ah! Jean-Jacques!' he readily concurs. 'Le pauvre,' he adds.

He squints lugubriously down his museau.

'Une crise de foie. Hélas, il est mort.'

I blanche like an endive. He, being a perfect gentleman, offers me a restorative snifter of his bubbly, brought as it has been all the way from his own cellars, he don't trust Sir's incinerated tastes, and I can feel it put hairs on my chest as it goes eructating down. Primed by another bottle, in which the duc joins me with that easy democratic affability which is the mark of all true aristocrats, I give him an account of what I take to be the circumstances of my conception, how his defunct valet wooed and won my mother in the course of the cooking of a lobster soufflé.

'I well remember that soufflé,' says the duc. 'Best I ever eat. Sent my compliments to the chef by way of the concierge, only added the advice of a truly exigeant gourmet to go easy on the cayenne, next time.'

So that was the truth of it! The spiteful housekeeper relaying only half the message!

I then relate the touching story, how, every Grouse Shoot after, my mother puts up a lobster soufflé in (I believe) remembrance of Jean-Jacques, and we share another bottle of bubbly in memory of the departed until the duc, exhibiting all the emotion of a tender sensibility, says through a manly tear:

'Tell you what, me lad, while your maman is once again fixing me up this famous lobster soufflé, I shall myself, as a tribute to my ex-valet, slip down –'

'Oh, sir!' I stammer. 'You are too good!'

Forthwith I speed to the kitchen to find my mother just beginning the bechamel. Presently, as the butter melts like the heart of the duc melted when I told him her tale, the kitchen door steals open and in tippytoes Himself. Never a couple better matched for size, I must say. The kitchen battalion all turn their heads away, out of respect for this romantic moment, but I myself, the architect of it, cannot forbear to peep.

He creeps up behind her, his index finger pressed to his lips to signify caution and silence, and extends his arm, and, slowly, slowly, slowly, with infinite delicacy and tact, he lets his hand adventure athwart her flank. It might have been a fly alighting on her bum. She flicks a haunch, like a mare in the field, unmoved, shakes in the flour. The duc himself quivers a bit. An expression as of a baby in a sweetie shop traverses his somewhat Bourbonesque features. He is attempting to peer over her shoulder to see what she is up to with her *batterie de cuisine* but his *embonpoint* gets in the way.

Perhaps it is to shift her over a bit, or else a genuine tribute to her large charms, but now, with immense if gigantic grace, he *gooses* her.

My mother fetches out a sigh, big enough to blow away the beaten egg-whites but, great artist that she is, her hand never trembles, not once, as she folds in the yolks. And when the ducal hands stray higher – not a mite of agitation stirs the spoon.

For it is, you understand, the time for seasoning. And in goes just sufficient cayenne, this time. Not a grain more. Huzzah! This soufflé will be – I flourish the circle I have made with my thumb and forefinger, I simulate a kiss.

The egg-whites topple into the panada; the movements of her spoon are quick and light as those of a bird caught in a trap. She upturns all into the soufflé dish.

He tweaks.

And *then* she cries: 'To hell with it!' Departing from the script, my mother wields her wooden spoon like a club, brings it, smack! down on to the duc's head with considerable force. He drops on to the flags with a low moan.

'Take that,' she bids his prone form. Then she smartly shuts the soufflé in the oven.

'How could you!' I cry.

'Would you have him spoil my soufflé? Wasn't it touch and go, last time?'

The grinding boy and I get the duc up on the marble slab, slap his face, dab his temples with the oven cloth dipped in chilled chablis, at long last his eyelids flicker, he comes to.

'Quelle femme,' he murmurs.

My mother, crouching over the range stopwatch in hand, pays him no heed.

'She feared you'd spoil the soufflé,' I explain, overcome with embarrassment.

'What dedication!'

The man seems awestruck. He stares at my mother as if he will never get enough of gazing at her. Bounding off the marble slab as sprightly as a man his size may, he hurls himself across the kitchen, falls on his knees at her feet.

'I beg you, I implore you –'

But my mother has eyes only for the oven.

'*Here* you are!' Throwing open the door, she brings forth the veritable queen of all the soufflés, that spreads its archangelic wings over the entire kitchen as it leaps upwards from the dish in which the force of gravity alone confines it. All present (some forty-seven in number – the kitchen brigade with the addition of me, plus the duc) applaud and cheer.

The housekeeper is mad as fire when my mother goes off in the closed barouche to the duc's very own regal and French kitchen but she comforts herself with the notion that now she can persuade Sir and Madam to find her a spanking new chef such as Soyer or Carême to twirl their moustaches in her direction and *gateau Saint-Honoré* her on her birthday and indulge her in not infrequent *babas au rhum*. But – I am the only child of my mother's kitchen and now I enter into my inheritance; besides, how can the housekeeper complain? Am I not the youngest (Yorkshire born) French chef in all the land?

For am I not the duc's stepson?

Black Venus

———

Sad; so sad, those smoky-rose, smoky-mauve evenings of late Autumn, sad enough to pierce the heart. The sun departs the sky in winding sheets of gaudy cloud; anguish enters the city, a sense of the bitterest regret, a nostalgia for things we never knew, anguish of the turn of the year, the time of impotent yearning, the inconsolable season. In America, they call it 'the Fall', bringing to mind the Fall of Man, as if the fatal drama of the primal fruit-theft must recur again and again, with cyclic regularity, at the same time of every year that schoolboys set out to rob orchards, invoking, in the most everyday image, any child, every child, who, offered the choice between virtue and knowledge, will always choose knowledge, always the hard way. Although she does not know the meaning of the word, 'regret', the woman sighs, without any precise reason.

Soft twists of mist invade the alleys, rise up from the slow river like exhalations of an exhausted spirit, seep in through the cracks in the window frames so that the contours of their high, lonely apartment waver and melt. On these evenings, you see everything as though your eyes are going to lapse to tears.

She sighs.

The custard-apple of her stinking Eden she, this forlorn Eve, bit – and was all at once transported here, as in a dream; and yet she is a *tabula rasa*, still. She never experienced her experience *as* experience, life never added to the sum of her knowledge; rather, subtracted from it. If you start out with nothing, they'll take even that away from you, the Good Book says so.

Indeed, I think she never bothered to bite any apple at all. She wouldn't have known what knowledge was *for*, would she? She was in neither a state of innocence nor a state of grace. I will tell you what Jeanne was like.

She was like a piano in a country where everyone has had their hands cut off.

On these sad days, at those melancholy times, as the room sinks into dusk, he, instead of lighting the lamp, fixing drinks, making all cosy, will ramble on: 'Baby, baby, let me take you back where you belong, back to your lovely, lazy island where the jewelled parrot rocks on the enamel tree and you can crunch sugar-cane between your strong, white teeth, like you did when you were little, baby. When we get there, among the lilting palm-trees, under the purple flowers, I'll love you to death. We'll go back and live together in a thatched house with a veranda over-grown with flowering vine and a little girl in a short white frock with a yellow satin bow in her kinky pigtail will wave a huge feather fan over us, stirring the languishing air as we sway in our hammock, this way and that way . . . the ship, the ship is waiting in the harbour, baby. My monkey, my pussy-cat, my pet . . . think how lovely it would be to live there . . .'

But, on these days, nipped by frost and sulking, no pet nor pussy she; she looks more like an old crow with rusty feathers in a miserable huddle by the smoky fire which she pokes with spiteful sticks. She coughs and grumbles, she is always chilly, there is always a draught gnawing the back of her neck or pinching her ankles.

Go, where? Not *there*! The glaring yellow shore and harsh blue sky daubed in crude, unblended colours squeezed directly from the tube, where the perspectives are abrupt as a child's drawing, your eyes hurt to look. Fly-blown towns. All there is to eat is green bananas and yams and a brochette of rubber goat to chew. She puts on a theatrical shudder, enough to shake the affronted cat off her lap. She hates the cat, anyway. She can't look at the cat without wanting to strangle it. She would like a drink. Rum will do. She twists a flute of discarded manuscript from the waste-paper basket into a spill for her small, foul, black cheroot.

Night comes in on feet of fur and marvellous clouds drift past the windows, those spectral clouds of the night sky that are uncannily visible when no light is there. The whim of the master of the house has not let the windows alone; he had all the panes except the topmost ones replaced with frosted glass so that the inmates could pursue an uninterrupted view of the sky as if they were living in the gondola of a balloon such as the one in which his friend Nadar made triumphant ascents.

At the inspiration of a gust of wind such as now rattles the tiles above us, this handsome apartment with its Persian rugs, its walnut table off which the Borgias served poisons, its carved armchairs from whose bulbous legs grin and grimace cinquecento faces, the crust of fake Tintorettos on the walls (he's an indefatigable connoisseur, if, as yet, too young to have that sixth sense that tells you when you're being conned) – at the invitation of the mysterious currents of the heavens, this well-appointed cabin will loose its moorings in the street below and take off, depart, whisk across the dark vault of the night, tangling a stillborn, crescent moon in its ropes, nudging a star at lift-off, and will deposit us –

'*No!*' she said. 'Not the bloody parrot forest! Don't take me on the slavers' route back to the West Indies, for godsake! And let the bloody cat out, before it craps on your precious Bokhara!'

They have this in common, neither has a native land, although he likes to pretend she has a fabulous home in the bosom of a blue ocean, he will force a home on her whether she's got one or not, he cannot believe she is as dispossessed as he is . . . Yet they are only at home together when contemplating flight; they are both waiting for the wind to blow that will take them to a miraculous elsewhere, a happy land, far, far away, the land of delighted ease and pleasure.

After she's got a drink or two inside her, however, she stops coughing, grows a bit more friendly, will consent to unpin her hair and let him play with it, the way he likes to. And, if her native indolence does not prove too much for her – for she is capable of sprawling, as in a vegetable trance, for hours, for days, in the dim room by the smoky fire – nevertheless, she will sometimes lob the butt of her cheroot in the fire and be persuaded to take off her clothes and dance for Daddy who, she will grudgingly admit when pressed, is a good Daddy, buys her pretties, allocates her the occasional lump of hashish, keeps her off the street.

Nights of October, of frail, sickle moons, when the earth conceals the shining accomplice of assassins in its shadow, to make everything all the more mysterious – on such a night, you could say the moon was black.

This dance, which he wanted her to perform so much and had especially devised for her, consisted of a series of voluptuous poses one following another; private-room-in-a-bordello stuff but tasteful, he preferred her to undulate rhythmically rather than jump about and shake a leg. He liked her to put on all her bangles and beads when she did her dance, she dressed up in the set of clanking jewellery he'd given her, paste, nothing she could sell or she'd have sold it. Meanwhile, she hummed a Créole melody, she liked the ones with ribald words about what the shoemaker's wife did at Mardi Gras or the size of some fisherman's legendary tool but Daddy paid no attention to what song his siren sang, he fixed his quick, bright, dark eyes upon her decorated skin as if, sucker, authentically entranced.

'Sucker!' she said, almost tenderly, but he did not hear her.

She cast a long shadow in the firelight. She was a woman of immense height, the type of those beautiful giantesses who, a hundred years later, would grace the stages of the Crazy Horse or the Casino de Paris in sequin cache-sexe and tinsel pasties, divinely tall, the colour and texture of suede. Josephine Baker! But vivacity, exuberance were never Jeanne's qualities. A slumbrous resentment of anything you could not eat, drink or smoke, i.e. burn, was her salient characteristic. Consumption, combustion, these were her vocations.

She sulked sardonically through Daddy's sexy dance, watching, in a bored, fascinated way, the elaborate reflections of the many strings of glass beads he had given her tracking about above her on the ceiling. She looked like the source of light but this was an illusion; she only shone because the dying fire lit his presents to her. Although his regard made her luminous, his shadow made her blacker than she was, his shadow could eclipse her entirely. Whether she had a good heart or not underneath, is anybody's guess; she had been raised in the School of Hard Knocks and enough hard knocks can beat the heart out of anybody.

Though Jeanne was not prone to introspection, sometimes, as she wriggled around the dark, buoyant room that tugged at its moorings, longing to take off on an aerial quest for that Cythera beloved of poets, she wondered what the distinction was between dancing naked in front of *one* man who paid and dancing naked in front of a group of men who paid. She had the impression that, somewhere in the difference, lay morality. Tutors in the School of Hard Knocks, that is, other chorus girls in the cabaret, where, in her sixteenth summer, she had tunelessly croaked these same Créole ditties she now hummed, had told her there was all the difference in the world and, at sixteen, she could conceive of no higher ambition than to be kept; that is, kept off the streets. Prostitution was a question of number; of being paid by more than one person at a time. That was bad. She was not a bad girl. When she slept with anyone else but Daddy, she never let them pay. It was a matter of honour. It was a question of fidelity. (In these ethical surmises slumbered the birth of irony although her lover assumed she was promiscuous because she *was* promiscuous.)

Now, however, after a few crazy seasons in the clouds with him, she sometimes asked herself if she'd played her cards right. If she was going to have to dance naked to earn her keep, anyway, why shouldn't she dance naked for hard cash in hand and earn enough to keep herself? Eh? Eh?

But then, the very thought of organising a new career made her yawn. Dragging herself around madames and music halls and so on; what an effort. And how much to ask? She had only the haziest notion of her own use value.

She danced naked. Her necklaces and earrings clinked. As always, when she finally got herself up off her ass and started dancing, she quite enjoyed it. She felt almost warm towards him; her good luck he was young and handsome. Her bad luck his finances were rocky, the opium, the scribbling; that he . . . but, at 'that', she snapped her mind off.

Thinking resolutely of her good luck, she held out her hands to her lover, flashed her teeth at him – the molars might be black stumps, already, but the pointed canines still white as vampires' – and invited him to join in and dance with her. But he never would, never. Scared of muzzing his shirt or busting his collar or something, even if, when stoned, he would clap his hands to the rhythm. She liked it when he did that. She felt he was appreciating her. After a few drinks, she forgot the other thing altogether, although she guessed, of course. The girls told over the ghoulish litany of the symptoms together in the dressing-room in hushed, scared voices, peeking at the fortune-telling mirror and seeing, not their rosy faces, but their own rouged skulls.

When she was on her own, having a few drinks in front of the fire, thinking about it, it made her break out in a horrible hag's laughter, as if she were already the hag she would become enjoying a grim joke at the expense of the pretty, secretly festering thing she still was. At Walpurgisnacht, the young witch boasted to the old witch: 'Naked on a goat, I display my fine young body.' How the old witch laughed! 'You'll rot!' I'll rot, thought Jeanne, and laughed. This cackle of geriatric cynicism ill became such a creature made for pleasure as Jeanne, but was pox not the emblematic fate of a creature made for pleasure and the price you paid for the atrocious mixture of corruption and innocence this child of the sun brought with her from the Antilles?

For herself, she came clean, arrived in Paris with nothing worse than scabies, malnutrition and ringworm about her person. It was a bad joke, therefore, that, some centuries before Jeanne's birth, the Aztec goddess, Nanahuatzin, had poured a cornucopia of wheelchairs, dark glasses, crutches and mercury pills on the ships of the conquistadores as they took their spoiled booty from the New World to the Old; the raped continent's revenge, perpetrating itself in the beds of Europe. Jeanne innocently followed Nanahuatzin's trail across the Atlantic but she brought no erotic vengeance – she'd picked up the germ from the very first protector. The man she'd trusted to take her away from all that, enough to make a horse laugh, except that she was a fatalist, she was indifferent.

She bent over backwards until the huge fleece of a black sheep, her unfastened hair, spilled on to the Bokhara. She was a supple acrobat; she could make her back into a mahogany rainbow. (Notice her big feet and huge, strong hands, capable enough to have been a nurse's hands.) If he was a connoisseur of the beautiful, she was a connoisseur of the most exquisite humiliations but she had always been too poor to be able to afford the luxury of acknowledging a humiliation as such. You took what came. She arched her back so much a small boy could have run under her. Her reversed blood sang in her ears.

Upside down as she was, she could see, in the topmost right-hand window-pane he had left unfrosted, the sickle moon, precise as if pasted on the sky. This moon was the size of a broad nail-paring; you could see the vague outline of the rest of its surface, obscured by the shadow of the earth as if the earth were clenched between the moon's shining claw-tips, so you could say the moon held the world in its arms. An exceptionally brilliant star suspended from the nether prong on a taut, invisible leash.

The basalt cat, the pride of the home, its excretory stroll along the quai concluded, now whined for readmittance outside the door. The poet let Puss in. Puss leapt into his waiting arms and filled the apartment with a happy purr. The girl plotted to strangle the cat with her long, agile toes but, indulgent from the exercise of her sensuality, she soon laughed to see him loving up the cat with the same gestures, the same endearments, he used on her. She forgave the cat for its existence; they had a lot in common. She released the bow of her back with a twang and plumped on the rug, rubbing her stretched tendons.

He said she danced like a snake and she said, snakes can't dance:

they've got no legs, and he said, but kindly, you're an idiot, Jeanne; but she knew he'd never so much as *seen* a snake, nobody who'd seen a snake move – that quick system of transverse strikes, lashing itself like a whip, leaving a rippling snake in the sand behind it, terribly fast – if he'd seen a snake move, he'd never have said a thing like that. She huffed off and contemplated her sweating breasts; she would have liked a bath, anyway, she was a little worried about a persistent vaginal discharge that smelled of mice, something new, something ominous, something horrid. But: no hot water, not at this hour.

'They'll bring up hot water if you pay.'

His turn to sulk. He took to cleaning his nails again.

'You think I don't need to wash because I don't show the dirt.'

But, even as she launched the first darts of a shrew's assault that she could have protracted for a tense, scratchy hour or more, had she been in the mood, she lost the taste for it. She was seized with sudden indifference. What does it matter? we're all going to die; we're as good as dead already. She drew her knees up to her chin and crouched in front of the fire, staring vacantly at the embers. Her face fixed in sullen resentment. The cat drew silently alongside, as if on purpose, adding a touch of satanic glamour, so you could imagine both were having silent conversations with the demons in the flames. As long as the cat left her alone, she let it alone. They were alone together. The quality of the separate self-absorptions of the cat and the woman was so private that the poet felt outmanoeuvred and withdrew to browse in his bookshelves, those rare, precious volumes, the jewelled missals, the incunabula, those books acquired from special shops that incurred damnation if you so much as opened the covers. He cherished his arduously aroused sexuality until she was prepared to acknowledge it again.

He thinks she is a vase of darkness; if he tips her up, black light will spill out. She is not Eve but, herself, the forbidden fruit, and he has eaten her!

Weird goddess, dusky as night,
  reeking of musk smeared on tobacco,
  a shaman conjured you, a Faust of the savannah,
  black-thighed witch, midnight's child.

Indeed, the Faust who summoned her from the abyss of which her eyes retain the devastating memory must have exchanged her presence for his soul; black Helen's lips suck the marrow from the poet's spirit, although she wishes to do no such thing. Apart from her meals and a few drinks, she is without many conscious desires. If she were a Buddhist, she would be halfway on the road to sainthood because she wants so little, but, alas, she is still pricked by needs.

The cat yawned and stretched. Jeanne woke from her trance. Folding another spill out of a dismantled sonnet to ignite a fresh cheroot, her bib of cut glass a-jingle and a-jangle, she turned to the poet to ask, in her inimitable half-raucous, half-caressing voice, voice of a crow reared on honey, with its dawdling accent of the Antilles, for a little money.

Nobody seems to know in what year Jeanne Duval was born, although the year in which she met Charles Baudelaire (1842) is precisely logged and the biographies of his other mistresses, Aglaé-Josephine Sabatier and Marie Daubrun, are well documented. Besides Duval, she also used the names Prosper and Lemer, as if her name was of no consequence. Where she came from is a problem; books suggest Mauritius, in the Indian ocean, or Santo Domingo, in the Caribbean, take your pick of two different sides of the world. (Her *pays d'origine* of less importance than it would have been had she been a wine.) Mauritius looks like a shot in the dark based on the fact that Baudelaire spent some time on that island during his abortive trip to India in 1841. Santo Domingo, Columbus' Hispaniola, now the Dominican Republic, a troubled history, borders upon Haiti. Here Toussaint L'Ouverture led a successful slave revolt against French plantation owners at the time of the French Revolution.

Although slavery had been abolished without debate throughout the French possessions by the National Assembly in 1794, it was reimposed in Martinique and Guadeloupe – though not in Haiti – by Napoleon. These slaves were not finally emancipated until 1848. However, African mistresses of French residents were often manumitted, together with their children, and intermarriage was by no means a rare occurrence. A middle-class Créole population grew up; to this class belonged the Josephine who became Empress of the French on her marriage to the same Napoleon.

It is unlikely that Jeanne Duval belonged to this class if, in fact, she came from Martinique, which, since she seems to have been Francophone, remains a possibility.

He made a note in 'Mon Coeur Mis à Nu': 'Of the People's hatred of

Beauty. Examples: Jeanne and Mme Muller.' (Who was Mme Muller?)

Kids in the street chucked stones at her, she so tall and witchy and, when she was pissed, teetering along with the vulnerable, self-conscious dignity of the drunk which always invites mockery, and, always, she held her bewildered head with its enormous, unravelling cape of hair as proudly as if she were carrying upon it an enormous pot full of all the waters of Lethe. Maybe he found her crying because the kids in the street were chucking stones at her, calling her a 'black bitch' or worse and spattering the beautiful white flounces of her crinoline with handfuls of tossed mud they scooped from the gutters where they thought she belonged because she was a whore who had the nerve to sashay to the corner shop for cheroots or *ordinaire* or rum with her nose stuck up in the air as if she were the Empress of all the Africas.

But she was the deposed Empress, royalty in exile, for, of the entire and heterogeneous wealth of all those countries, had she not been dispossessed?

Robbed of the bronze gateways of Benin; of the iron breasts of the amazons of the court of the King of Dahomey; of the esoteric wisdom of the great university of Timbuktu; of the urbanity of glamorous desert cities before whose walls the horsemen wheel, welcoming the night on trumpets twice the length of their own bodies. The Abyssinia of black saints and holy lions was not even so much as a legend to her. Of those savannahs where men wrestle with leopards she knew not one jot. The splendid continent to which her skin allied her had been excised from her memory. She had been deprived of history, she was the pure child of the colony. The colony – white, imperious – had fathered her. Her mother went off with the sailors and her granny looked after her in one room with a rag-covered bed.

Her granny said to Jeanne: 'I was born in the ship where my mother died and was thrown into the sea. Sharks ate her. Another woman of some other nation who had just still-born suckled me. I don't know anything about my father nor where I was conceived nor on what coast nor in what circumstances. My foster-mother soon died of fever in the plantation. I was weaned. I grew up.'

Nevertheless, Jeanne retained a negative inheritance; if you tried to get her to do anything she didn't want to, if you tried to erode that little steely nugget of her free will, which expressed itself as lethargy, you could see how she had worn away the patience of the missionaries and so come to inherit, not even self-pity, only the twenty-nine legally permitted strokes of the whip.

Her granny spoke Créole, patois, knew no other language, spoke it badly and taught it badly to Jeanne, who did her best to convert it into good French when she came to Paris and started mixing with swells but made a hash of it, her heart wasn't in it, no wonder. It was as though her tongue had been cut out and another one sewn in that did not fit well. Therefore you could say, not so much that Jeanne did not understand the lapidary, troubled serenity of her lover's poetry but, that it was a perpetual affront to her. He recited it to her by the hour and she ached, raged and chafed under it because his eloquence denied her language. It made her dumb, a dumbness all the more profound because it manifested itself in a harsh clatter of ungrammatical recriminations and demands which were not directed at her lover so much – she was quite fond of him – as at her own condition, great gawk of an ignorant black girl, good for nothing: correction, good for only one thing, even if the spirochetes were already burrowing away diligently at her spinal marrow while she bore up the superb weight of oblivion on her Amazonian head.

The greatest poet of alienation stumbled upon the perfect stranger; theirs was a match made in heaven. In his heart, he must have known this.

The goddess of his heart, the ideal of the poet, lay resplendently on the bed in a room morosely papered red and black; he liked to have her make a spectacle of herself, to provide a sumptuous feast for his bright eyes that were always bigger than his belly.

Venus lies on the bed, waiting for a wind to rise: the sooty albatross hankers for the storm. Whirlwind!

She was acquainted with the albatross. A scallop-shell carried her stark naked across the Atlantic; she clutched an enormous handful of dreadlocks to her pubic mound. Albatrosses hitched glides on the gales the wee black cherubs blew for her.

The Albatross can fly around the world in eight days, if only it sticks to the stormy places. The sailors call the huge birds ugly names, goonies, mollyhawks, because of their foolish clumsiness on the ground but wind, wind is their element; they have absolute mastery of it.

Down there, far down, where the buttocks of the world slim down again, if you go far south enough you reach again the realm of perpetual cold that begins and ends our experience on this earth, those ranges of ice mountains where the bull-roaring winds bay and bellow and no people are, only the stately penguin in his frock coat not unlike yours, Daddy, the estimable but, unlike you, uxorious penguin who balances the precious egg on his feet while his dear wife goes out and has as good a time as the Antarctic may afford.

If Daddy were like a penguin, how much more happy we should be; there isn't room for two albatrosses in *this* house.

Wind is the element of the albatross just as domesticity is that of the penguin. In the 'Roaring Forties' and 'Furious Fifties', where the high winds blow ceaselessly from west to east between the remotest tips of the inhabited continents and the blue nightmare of the uninhabitable ice, these great birds glide in delighted glee, south, far south, so far south it inverts the notional south of the poet's parrot-forest and glittering beach; down here, down south, only the phlegmatic mono-chrome, flightless birds form the audience for the wonderful *aerielistes* who live in the heart of the storm – like the bourgeoisie, Daddy, sitting good and quiet with their eggs on their feet watching artistes such as we dare death upon the high trapeze.

The woman and her lover wait for the rising of the wind upon which they will leave the gloomy apartment. They believe they can ascend and soar upon it. This wind will be like that from a new planet.

The young man inhales the aroma of the coconut oil which she rubs into her hair to make it shine. His agonised romanticism transforms this homely odour of the Caribbean kitchen into the perfume of the air of those tropical islands he can sometimes persuade himself are the happy lands for which he longs. His lively imagination performs an alchemical alteration on the healthy tang of her sweat, freshly awakened by dancing. He thinks her sweat smells of cinnamon because she has spices in her pores. He thinks she is made of a different kind of flesh than his.

It is essential to their connection that, if she should put on the private garments of nudity, its non-sartorial regalia of jewellery and rouge, then he himself must retain the public nineteenth-century masculine impedimenta of frock coat (exquisitely cut); white shirt (pure silk, London tailored); oxblood cravat; and impeccable trousers. There's more to 'Le Déjeuner sur l'Herbe' than meets the eye. (Manet, another friend of his.) Man does and is dressed to do so; his skin is his own business. He is artful, the creation of culture. Woman is; and is, therefore, fully dressed in no clothes at all, her skin is common property, she is a being at one with nature in a fleshly simplicity that, he insists, is the most abominable of artifices.

Once, before she became a kept woman, he and a group of Bohemians contrived to kidnap her from her customers at the cabaret, spirited her, at first protesting, then laughing, off with them, and they'd wandered along the streets in the small hours, looking for a place to take their prize for another drink and she urinated in the street, right there, didn't announce it; nor go off into an alley to do it on her own; she did not even leave go his arm but straddled the gutter, legs apart, and pissed as if it was the most natural thing in the world. Oh, the unexpected Chinese bells of that liquid cascade!

(At which point, his Lazarus arose and knocked unbidden on the coffin-lid of the poet's trousers.)

Jeanne hitched up her skirts with her free hand as she stepped across the pool she'd made, so that he saw where she had splashed her white stockings at the ankle. It seemed to his terrified, exacerbated sensibility that the liquid was a kind of bodily acid that burned away the knitted cotton, dissolved her petticoat, her stays, her chemise, the dress she wore, her jacket, so that now she walked beside him like an ambulant fetish, savage, obscene, terrifying.

He himself always wore gloves of pale pink kid that fitted as tenderly close as the rubber gloves that gynaecologists will wear. Watching him play with her hair, she tranquilly recollected a red-haired friend in the cabaret who had served a brief apprenticeship in a brothel but retired from the profession after she discovered a significant proportion of her customers wanted nothing more of her than permission to ejaculate into her magnificent Titian mane. (How the girls giggled over that.) The red-haired girl thought that, on the whole, this messy business was less distasteful and more hygienic than regular intercourse but it meant that she had to wash her hair so often that her crowning, indeed – she was a squint-eyed little thing – unique glory was stripped of its essential, natural oils. Seller and commodity in one, a whore is her own investment in the world and so she must take care of herself; the squinting red-head decided she dare not risk squandering her capital so recklessly but Jeanne never had this temperament of the tradesperson, she did not feel she was her own property and so she gave herself away to everybody except the poet, for whom she had too much respect to offer such an ambivalent gift for nothing.

'Get it up for me,' said the poet.

'Albatrosses are famous for the courtship antics they carry on throughout the breeding season. These involve grotesque, awkward dancing, accompanied by bowing, scraping, snapping of bills, and prolonged nasal groans.'

Birds of the World, Oliver L. Austin Jnr

They are not great nest builders. A slight depression in the ground will do. Or, they might hollow out a little mound of mud. They will make only the most squalid concessions to the earth. He envisaged their bed, the albatross's nest, as just such a fleeting kind of residence in which Destiny, the greatest madame of all, had closeted these two strange birds together. In this transitory exile, anything is possible.

'Jeanne, get it up for me.'

Nothing is simple for this fellow! He makes a performance worthy of the Comédie Française out of a fuck, bringing him off is a five act drama with farcical interludes and other passages that could make you cry and, afterwards, cry he does, he is ashamed, he talks about his mother, but Jeanne can't remember her mother and her granny swapped her with a ship's mate for a couple of bottles, a bargain with which her granny said she was well satisfied because Jeanne was already getting into trouble and growing out of her clothes and ate so much.

While they had been untangling together the history of transgression, the fire went out; also, the small, white, shining, winter moon in the top left-hand corner of the top left-hand pane of the few sheets of clear glass in the window had, accompanied by its satellite star, completed the final section of its low arc over the black sky. While Jeanne stoically laboured over her lover's pleasure, as if he were her vineyard, she laying up treasure in heaven from her thankless toil, moon and star arrived together at the lower right-hand window-pane.

If you could see her, if it were not so dark, she would look like the victim of a robbery; her bereft eyes are like abysses but she will hold him to her bosom and comfort him for betraying to her in his self-disgust those trace elements of common humanity he has left inside her body, for which he blames her bitterly, for which he will glorify her, awarding her the eternity promised by the poet.

The moon and star vanish.

Nadar says he saw her a year or so after, deaf, dumb and paralysed, Baudelaire died. The poet, finally, so far estranged from himself that, in the last months before the disease triumphed over him, when he was shown his reflection in a mirror, he bowed politely, as to a stranger. He told his mother to make sure that Jeanne was looked after but his mother didn't give her anything. Nadar says he saw Jeanne hobbling on crutches along the pavement to the dram-shop; her teeth were gone, she had a mammy-rag tied around her head but you could still see that her wonderful hair had fallen out. Her face would terrify the little children. He did not stop to speak to her.

The ship embarked for Martinique.

You can buy teeth, you know; you can buy hair. They make the best wigs from the shorn locks of novices in convents.

The man who called himself her brother, perhaps they *did* have the same mother, why not? She hadn't the faintest idea what had happened to her mother and this hypothetical, high-yellow, demi-sibling popped up in the nick of time to take over her disordered finances with the skill of a born entrepreneur – he might have been Mephistopheles, for all she cared. Her brother. They'd salted away what the poet managed to smuggle to her, all the time he was dying, when his mother wasn't looking. Fifty francs for Jeanne, here; thirty francs for Jeanne, there. It all added up.

She was surprised to find out how much she was worth.

Add to this the sale of a manuscript or two, the ones she hadn't used to light her cheroots with. Some books, especially the ones with the flowery dedications. Sale of cuff-links and drawerful upon drawerful of pink kid gloves, hardly used. Her brother knew where to get rid of them. Later, any memorabilia of the poet, even his clumsy drawings, would fetch a surprising sum. They left a portfolio with an enterprising agent.

In a new dress of black tussore, her somewhat ravaged but carefully repaired face partially concealed by a flattering veil, she chugged away from Europe on a steamer bound for the Caribbean like a respectable widow and she was not yet fifty, after all. She might have been the Créole wife of a minor civil servant setting off home after his death.

Her brother went first, to look out the property they were going to buy.

Her voyage was interrupted by no albatrosses. She never thought of the slavers' route, unless it was to compare her grandmother's crossing with her own, comfortable one. You could say that Jeanne had found herself; she had come down to earth, and, with the aid of her ivory cane, she walked perfectly well upon it. The sea air did her good. She decided to give up rum, except for a single tot last thing at night, after the accounts were completed.

See her, now, in her declining years, every morning in decent black, leaning a little on her stick but stately as only one who has snatched herself from the lion's mouth can be. She leaves the charming house, with its vine-covered verandah; 'Good morning, Mme Duval!' sings out the obsequious gardener. How sweet it sounds. She is taking last night's takings to the bank. 'Thank you so much, Mme Duval.' As soon as she had got her first taste of it, she became a glutton for deference.

Until at last, in extreme old age, she succumbs to the ache in her bones and a cortège of grieving girls takes her to the churchyard, she will continue to dispense, to the most privileged of the colonial administration, at a not excessive price, the veritable, the authentic, the true Baudelairean syphilis.

The lines on page 117 are translated from:

SED NON SATIATA

Bizarre déité, brune comme les nuits,
Au parfum mélangé de musc et de havane,
Oeuvre de quelque obi, le Faust de la savane,
Sorcière au flanc d'ébène, enfant des noirs minuits,

Je préfère au constance, à l'opium, au nuits,
L'élixir de ta bouche où l'amour se pavane;
Quand vers toi mes désirs partent en caravane,
Tes yeux sont la citerne où boivent mes ennuis.

Par ces deux grands yeux noirs, soupiraux de ton âme,
Ô démon sans pitié! verse-moi moins de flamme;
Je ne suis pas le Styx pour t'embrasser neuf fois,

Hélas! et je ne puis, Mégère libertine,
Pour briser ton courage et te mettre aux abois,
Dans l'enfer de ton lit devenir Proserpine!

Les Fleurs du Mal, Charles Baudelaire

The other poems in *Les Fleurs du Mal* believed to have been written about Jeanne Duval, are often called the *'Black Venus cycle'*, and include: *'Les Bijoux'*, *'La Chevelure'*, *'Le Serpent qui danse'*, *'Parfum Exotique'*, *'Le Chat'*, *'Je t'adore à l'égal de la voûte nocturne'*, etc.